PRAISE FOR JAMES SCOTT BELL

A master of the cliffhanger, creating scene after scene of
mounting suspense and revelation . . . Heart-whamming.

— **PUBLISHERS WEEKLY**

A master of suspense.

— **LIBRARY JOURNAL**

One of the best writers out there, bar none.

— **IN THE LIBRARY REVIEW**

There'll be no sleeping till after the story is over.

— **JOHN GILSTRAP**, NYT BESTSELLING
AUTHOR

James Scott Bell's writing is as sharp as a switchblade.

— **MEG GARDINER**, EDGAR AWARD
WINNING AUTHOR

A storyteller in the tradition of the great thriller masters.

— **TOSCA LEE**, NYT BESTSELLING AUTHOR

LAST CALL

JAMES SCOTT BELL

Published by Compendium Press
Los Angeles, CA

Courage is the price that life exacts for granting peace.

— AMELIA EARHART

Cats and monkeys, monkeys and cats — all human life is there.

— HENRY JAMES

CHAPTER ONE

"PINKY?"

He didn't answer.

"Pinky, come on, time to get up, honey."

He didn't move.

Keely shook her head. Why did they always do this? Think they could get just one more ride on the carousel without paying for a ticket?

The only thing she could think of was that most of her customers were high-end corporate types and professionals, men used to getting their way through force of will and bumping their gums. She gave them their way, of course. That's what they paid for. Even when they were fat, balding and with an overwhelmingly generous view of themselves and their place in the world. Keely knew how to make them feel slim, thirty, and a titan of industry.

But a freebie was not part of the package.

Pinky was actually one of the least obnoxious of her regulars. *Pinky*. Ha. They never used real names—usually it was Jack or Jerry or Steve. For some reason, this one liked to be called Pinky. It made him smile, especially when she whispered it in his ear.

"Time's a-wasting. Come on now." Keely was fixing her makeup at the mirror on the wall, looking at his reflection. She was suddenly taken aback by the juxtaposition of images.

She was twenty-five and her body, modified to be sure, was a sculpted male fantasy. Her blonde hair, worn like Marilyn Monroe, was a retro throwback that was all the rage now in call-girl circles. Keely herself had started the trend with a movie executive who then recommended her to, it seemed, all the straight men in his contacts list.

And there in the bed lay Pinky, blankets at mid torso, revealing a fleshy field of white hairs, like a shag carpet. He must have had quite a manly chest back in the day, which would have been about thirty years ago.

Now, looking at her own image and that of her blissfully sleeping client, she made another calculation. She had maybe five good years left at this. Then what? Go into business, like Madame V? Get a real job? Right. She hadn't finished high school. What chance did she have, as her mother had once said, of making her way in the world with head held high?

She got annoyed then. Every extra minute spent with this free rider now was a minute taken from what was left of her life.

She had no idea what that life would be, or even was, but it was *hers*.

Pulling on her red dress—Pinky always requested red—Keely turned from the mirror and made her way to the side of the bed.

"Now, Pinky," she said.

His face did not twitch.

In fact, its normally ruddy tones had disappeared. Now there was a dull grayness to the skin. His lips were the color of old plums.

Which was when the first chill winds of disquiet blew inside her.

"Pinky?"

Nothing.

She grabbed his jaw. His face was cold to the touch. She turned his head from side to side.

And then Keely Delmonico—the former Rachel Fisk of Bismarck, North Dakota—backed away from the bed and tried to catch her breath.

No, no, this couldn't be happening.

Yes it could. It happened to another of the girls, her friend Ynez, a couple of years ago. And what a mess it was. Police, three days in the jug. Almost a filing for manslaughter. Madam V had some sort of pull that got her out of it, but the result was Ynez had to leave L.A. altogether. She was somewhere in Nevada now.

But it had never happened to Keely! And what it would mean was cops and detectives and reporters, and she'd be all over the freaking internet and they'd dig into her life and tear it all apart.

Come on now, think! That's what you used to be good at, remember? You used to read and do puzzles, you used to do crosswords and Sudoku before they started in on you. Don't let them take that away. Think!

His phone. The cops could find her and Madam V through his phone. And then they'd make life miserable. It wasn't like it was back in the day when Madam V was going out. Back then you could get a cop to turn his head for some cash on the side and maybe a little something extra. Not anymore. Every single cop was scared to even sneeze wrong, lest they be caught on video.

There was another reason for the phone. Pinky had said something about making her an offer, a big deal. Something involving a lot of money, potentially. She'd taken that with a shaker of salt. But now she was curious. If it wasn't going to be too much trouble, maybe she could find out what that deal was.

Pinky's pants were folded on the sofa. Crisp black slacks with a black leather belt.

Front pockets. Keys, a money clip—healthy money clip, he always paid cash.

His coat was tossed over a chair. He'd done that himself when they first got in the room. He tossed it like a toreador throwing a flower to the crowd, and he laughed. It was something he did every time.

The jacket had his phone. A Samsung.

Keely pressed the button then swiped the screen. Good. No security. Pinky was old school.

Someone knocked on the door.

"Housekeeping," a tiny voice said.

What? Hadn't they put out the *Do Not Disturb* sign?

Another knock. "Housekeeping."

Keely said nothing.

The door clicked open.

CHAPTER TWO

THE SECURITY LOCK was in place—thank goodness—and the door clacked with only an inch of space open.

No way to avoid it now.

But Keely could at least try her *basso profundo*. When she was little she used to amuse her friend Cindy with her deep voice impressions of Matt LeBlanc and Kiefer Sutherland. It always made them both crack up. Because it sounded just like a girl trying to do a man's voice.

"Not now," Keely said, with a bit of a whispered snarl.

"Oh, I am sorry!" the maid said.

The door closed.

Back to business. Get out of here. Take the phone. It could come in handy if they went over the room and found her abundant DNA mixed in with his.

Or would they get suspicious if they didn't find him with a phone?

Or a wallet.

She was thinking like a detective now, like in those Agatha Christies her grandmother had that Keely plowed through before the bad things started.

She put the phone in her handbag, helped herself to five crisp hundreds from the money clip.

Then she took a breath, went to the door, looked through the peep hole.

A housekeeping cart was at the door across from hers. The door was propped open.

Keely unclasped the lock and opened the door half way. She heard water running in the bathroom of the open room. She put the *Do Not Disturb* sign on the outside of the door, closed it, and walked fast to the elevator.

She paid for her parking at the machine, then drove her ruby-red Elantra up Figueroa to Sunset, turned left, and pointed toward home—Silver Lake. She had a nice apartment on Reservoir Street, and neighbors who thought she was in the film business.

In an odd way, she was. Films were about dreams, right? She made some dreams come true.

It was a little after eight when she got to her place. She stripped off her professional wear and took a shower. She dressed in a white sweatshirt and jeans and Converse sneakers.

Now she needed coffee.

And a cigarette.

But more than anything, she needed Amy.

parted on one side, and her small, taut body seemed coiled like a ninja warrior. Amy Matsumoto would've been right at home in a martial arts movie. She always seemed to be flying around the coffee bar, with attitude, ready to kick a rude customer right in his coffee cups.

Keely realized her hands were shaking and she put them together and held them in her lap. Laptop Satan was still looking at her, so she moved her chair around so her back was to him and she could look out the window.

She could see by the streetlights the homeless encampment near the freeway. She'd heard on the news that in Silver Lake violent crime was up about twenty-five percent. The city was going to hell, so maybe Laptop Satan was a real estate agent for the devil himself.

She really needed a cigarette.

She needed out of this town, but where could she go? Not back to home base, even though her grandmother still lived there and would certainly put her up. But the memories were too raw and the hometown cops would certainly want to grill her about the—

"Hey kid."

Keely jolted. Amy stood there, smiling, wearing a powder blue apron with the Cognoscenti logo on it.

"Jumpy," Amy said. "You okay?"

"Can we talk?" Keely said.

"What is it, hon?"

"You have a cigarette?"

"Not for you," Amy said.

"Come on."

"I'm not going to be your pusher. You quit, remember?"

"Talk. Out back. Can we?"

"I break in ten minutes. Can you wait?"

"I'll have to," Keely said.

"You really look bummed."

"It's more than that."

"I'll get you some chamomile," Amy said.

CHAPTER THREE

THE COGNOSCENTI WAS an upscale coffee bar and performance space on Sunset. Keely walked in and took a table near the front window. She did not want to be approached for anything other than a coffee order.

The place was a buzz of activity, a hive of the young-and-cool whose median age was about her own. It had a glossy concrete floor, red walls, aqua-marine chairs. There were group tables, doubles, and at least two intensely serious males leaning over laptops writing screenplays, novels, poetry, blogs, comments on other blogs, or emails to friends telling them how boss it was to be sipping joe in Silver Lake when most people were just getting to work.

One of the scribes was skinny and wore a scarf around his neck. He had a pointy wisp of devil's beard. He glanced up from his machine and they locked eyes for a second.

Keely averted her gaze quickly and realized she was the only one in the place who was not either writing, reading, or with someone she could talk to.

She looked around for Amy. She spotted her behind the counter steaming some milk. Her black and hot-pink hair was

"And a cigarette."

Amy laughed and shook her head as she zipped away.

Laptop Satan said, "Need a smoke?"

The devil surely would have smokes. "Yes, I do," she said.

"I've got one. Want to go out back?"

"I'm actually with someone," she said. "But I'll take the cig."

"I don't see anybody with you." He smiled in what he no doubt thought was Charm Grin #3.

"I'm waiting," she said.

"We could wait together," he said.

"It's private."

He kept the smile locked and reached into his backpack and pulled out a silver cigarette case. He opened the case and got up from his table and stepped over to hers. He held the case out for her. She removed an unfiltered cigarette.

"Thank you," she said.

"Let's go have it out back," he said.

"Thanks again, but no."

"You look like you have some trouble. I'm good at listening."

"You've been really nice, but I'm not in the mood to talk."

"You want to talk to that server," he said.

"She's a friend."

"Let me be your friend?"

"No, thank you."

"Come on." He made a move toward the other chair.

"Yo," she said. "Go back to your table, okay?"

He stiffened and his smile melted into his beard. "Real friendly." He shook his head as he went back to his table. He turned his laptop around then sat with his back to her.

Just like the rest of the world.

THERE WAS a small patio area in the back, with three tables and space for an outdoor platform stage. This one wasn't in use tonight. That was usually reserved for Saturdays and open poetry readings.

Amy was still wearing her apron and she and Keely were sitting at the table furthest from the building. Keely had the cigarette in her mouth and had her hands open to Amy in a *What are you waiting for* gesture.

"Not gonna do it," Amy said.

"Give me a light, please," Keely said.

"Remember when you were chewing Nicorette like a chipmunk? No more. Come on. Talk to me."

Keely took a deep breath, snatched the cigarette out of her mouth and placed it on the table. She reached in her purse and took out Pinky's phone and laid it next to the cigarette.

"Why so shaky?" Amy said.

"Isn't life shaky as is?" Keely said.

"You're not kidding. My dad just told me to keep washing my hands because of China."

"What?"

"He's an epidemiologist, you know."

"What's that?"

"It's all about public health and preventing disease. He says there's something cooking in China, some kind of new flu, and it'll probably come here big time. So I have to be ready for it."

"Terrific. Another thing to worry about."

Amy shrugged. "So what's going on with you?"

Keely paused, looked at the cigarette. She reached for it, stopped, put her hand on the table and held it down with the other hand.

"One of them died on me," Keely said.

Amy's chin dropped half an inch.

"That's right," Keely said. "Went bye-bye right there while I was with him."

"During?"

"After."

Amy shook her head. Then she reached in the pocket of her

apron and pulled out a pack of Marlboro Lights and a Bic lighter. She removed a cigarette and nodded at the cigarette on the table. Keely picked it up and put it in her mouth. Amy lit both their fires.

They puffed in silence for a long moment.

Amy said, "What did you do?"

"My grandmother had a saying. She used to say, if you made a bad choice—*You buttered your bread, now jam it.* I buttered my bread a long time ago."

"So what are you saying?"

"I'm saying I'm toast." Keely laughed. "Hey, that's pretty good. Maybe I should go into comedy."

"So what do you do when ... something like that happens?"

"They don't give us a freaking playbook!" She picked up Pinky's phone. "This."

"Your phone?"

"His phone."

"You took it?"

"I want to know who he is. And I don't want to talk to the cops."

"So who was he?"

"I haven't looked yet. You're the expert in technical stuff."

Amy took a puff, blew out smoke. "Can't you just walk away from this?"

"I want to know who he was."

"Why does it matter?"

Keely said, "Because he said he was going to make me an offer."

"About what?"

"He died before he could tell me!"

"Bad timing," Amy said.

"So if I can find out ..." Keely tapped the phone with her index finger.

"Isn't that evidence or something?" Amy said.

"I don't know! All I know is—"

"Ladies." Laptop Satan was there, like he'd appeared out of the smoke of hell.

Keely said, "Hey!"

"I just—"

"I know what you *just,*" Keely said. "Get out of here."

"—I thought you'd like to know, there's a policeman inside asking for somebody named Keely."

CHAPTER FOUR

"I DON'T WANT TO talk to any cops," Keely said.

"Are you in trouble?" Laptop Satan said.

Keely rolled her eyes in a way she hoped would tell him to get lost. The only thing lost on him was the message. He stood still, smiling.

Amy said, "Let me go and see what's going on."

She got up and smoothed her apron and went back in the store.

"Really," Laptop Satan said, sitting down without being asked. "I know people. I know lawyers. My dad's a lawyer—"

Keely put her hand up. "It's not like that."

"Just trying to be helpful."

"All right, I appreciate that."

"Can I know your name?"

"Why?"

"Ah, come on. I'm Max."

He stuck out his hand.

Keely didn't move.

"Don't leave me hangin'," he said.

She wanted to leave him, period. But she'd spent enough time judging the character of men on a moment's notice that she concluded he was harmless enough. And he *had* given her the cigarette.

She raised her hand in a fist. He did the same. They bumped.

"What can I call you?" Max said.

The word *call* banged in her head like a Chinese gong. "Keely."

"Keely?"

"Anything wrong with that?"

"No, no. I like it. Where'd it come from?"

It came from me in order to help save my life. "My grandmother liked a singer named Keely Smith."

"Your grandmother named you?"

"Yeah."

"So what do you do, Keely?"

"I'm ... an actress."

"Yeah? Have I ever seen you in anything?"

"I doubt it."

"Have anything coming up?"

"Why?"

"I'd like to watch it."

Keely almost laughed. She had to press her lips hard.

Max said, "It's not porn, is it?"

"Can we stop this conversation right here?"

" 'Cause I've got no problem with that."

Suddenly, Keely wanted to find the nearest freeway overpass so she could dive off it. When was her last hopeful day? Probably that day with Grandma on the farm, and Keely got to ride the horse. Sky was an American Paint, brown with great white splotches. And whenever she was at Grandma's she would ride Sky and feed her sugar cubes, and dream about someday jumping her, maybe in the Olympics, like all those rich kids got to do. She would be the poor kid who showed them all. She and Sky.

And now the only jumping she wanted to do was off a bridge. Sky was long dead. Life itself was long dead.

Amy came out then and said, "Do you know someone named Traci Fears?"

"Yeah," Keely said. "What is it?"

"She's in the hospital."

County-USC Medical Center was in East Los Angeles, in the crook of the freeway elbow formed by the 5 and the 10. Keely parked her Elantra in the lot across the street. Max had offered to drive her, but it was the perfect moment to escape his annoying ways. She'd entrusted Amy with Pinky's phone.

Because now it was all about Traci.

Through the metal detectors, and to the information window she walked. She was given a visitor sticker and labyrinthine directions to the room where she found Traci Fears, the very first person she'd met when she came to Los Angeles.

Traci's face was not the one Keely had seen that first time. This Traci was bruised and battered. Her small, cute nose was twice its normal size. Her pretty eyes were puffy and her creamy cheeks black-and-blue.

Keely knew who'd done that and cursed his name as she approached, but Traci put her finger to her lips and shook her head.

"No, really," Keely said. "This is too much."

"Please."

"He's got to be put away."

Another shake of the head. Traci reached for Keely's hand. Keely gave it to her. Traci's grip was as slight as a child's.

"He doesn't mean it, really," Traci said.

"You stupid—"

"Nobody knows him the way I do."

"You can't let him do this!"

"Shh. Please."

"No, I won't *please*." Keely grabbed a chair and pulled it next to the bed. This was going to take some persuading. "The cops will pick him up and then you have to say what happened."

"I already told them," Traci said.

"You did?"

"I told them it was a homeless guy."

Keely looked at the ceiling.

"I can't ruin his life," Traci said.

"He's going to keep on doing this," Keely said.

"He won't." Traci's words were slow and thick through her swollen mouth. "He knows he's got to get it together."

"Dude, listen to me. All he knows is dollar signs. All he knows is Jimmy Hansen. And everybody, including you and any other girlfriend, has to kiss his feet."

"He doesn't have any other girlfriends."

Keely didn't have the heart to set her straight on that one.

CHAPTER FIVE

HER REAL NAME WAS Virginia Millicent Mayfair, of the Kansas City, Kansas Mayfairs, but Keely and all the girls knew her as Madam V. A former high-end call girl herself, she now ran a boutique ring going on thirty years. All out of her beach house in Venice, a surprise bequest in the will of a grateful movie producer.

Keely always loved coming here. There were skylights in every room and when it was sunny, like today, Keely could forget that she did most of her work in the dark. Growing up in North Dakota, she never got to see the real ocean. But she could here at The Beehive, as the girls called it. She could sit for hours on the second story balcony and just look at the water, listen to the waves, float away on daydreams.

But today was not one of those days. Today it was all business and advice from her employer, who opened the front door wide for her.

"Darling!" Madam V said, and held her arms out for Keely. Her hug was massive and warm, like Madam V herself. She wore a flowing black dress with an array of gold jewelry on her chest, wrists, fingers, and ears. Today it was gold danglers on each ear that tinkled with every move of her stylish head. Madam V never looked anything but perfectly coiffed and painted. "You never

know when the iceman cometh," she was fond of saying, "but if
he shows up looking for a date you want to be ready to melt
him."

With the smell of Madam V's signature potpourri filling her
nostrils, Keely followed the boss to the spacious living room, deco-
rated in a style Madam V called "Latin Lover." There were two
paintings of matadors on the wall, one depicting the moment-of-
truth just before the death-thrust of the sword. A persistent rumor
among the girls was that a famous Mexican torero killed himself
with his own estoque when Madam V refused to marry him. When
asked if it was true, Madam V would always answer with a wry
smile and one word—"Olé."

Madam V gestured toward a red wing-back chair and said, "Sit
down, my darling, and tell Madame V all about it."

More shaken than she thought she would be, Keely sat and
gripped the arms of the chair.

"You need a drink," Madam V said, stepping behind the
ambrosia maple bar. She placed a bottle of Stolichnaya on the
turquoise inlaid bar top and put out two highball glasses. She
poured a healthy slug of Stoli into each glass, added a snort of V-8
and a dash of Tabasco. With silver tongs she placed two ice cubes
into each glass and swirled around her mixture with a foot-long
silver bar spoon.

She flowed back across the room and sat opposite Keely,
handing her one of the glasses.

"To money," Madam V said, and they clinked.

Keely sipped modestly. She was not a heavy drinker.

Madam V, on the other hand, slammed down half her glass.

"Now," Madam V said upon finishing, "tell me just what
happened."

Keely told her. And by the time she finished the story, Madame
V had finished her drink.

Madam V said, "It happens. The point is what we do about it.
And what we do about it is zippo."

"No police?"

"Especially not the police. Our relationship is tenuous. I don't want to upset any apple carts. Do they have apple carts anymore?"

"I don't know," Keely said.

"I'm sure they don't. Can I freshen you?"

Keely shook her head.

Madam V went to prepare another drink, speaking as she did. "I miss the old days. I miss when more politicians and city police were regulars. One's negotiating position was so much stronger."

She paused to ice and stir, then rejoined Keely.

"You know, I got started in this business with the president of the Los Angeles County Board of Supervisors. My first call, I was set up in a room at the Biltmore. He had a lobster dinner delivered, champagne. I was the dessert."

"A county supervisor, eh? What was he like?"

"Let's just say his motion failed to pass."

Keely smiled.

"Plus, he didn't pay me. He said I actually owed him money. For the nice dinner, the nice room, the potential connections. And his company."

"Unbelievable!"

"Democrat," Madam V said.

Keely laughed.

"But he didn't get away with it. I'd set up a camera. Even then I knew I was going to turn this into a business. I wanted something for my scrapbook. Ha!"

Keely's boss was now nice and loose and holding court.

"I put a set of the photographs in a safe deposit box. I typed out a letter—do you remember typewriters, dear?—and told him just what would happen to those photos if he did not pay me my freight plus an extra two bills for my inconvenience. I had the letter hand-delivered, with instructions for the lad not to leave until he had the money in hand. Two hours later it was in my hands."

"So simple," Keely said.

"A week later I got a call from a prominent businessman here in town. A wheeler dealer, as they used to say. Took me to a nice dinner in Beverly Hills, then we went to his room at the Chateau Marmont. In the room was the Chief of Police of Los Angeles. The businessman left. He spoke to me very sternly. He said he'd heard a rumor about my blackmailing a county supervisor. I told him it wasn't blackmail, it was billing. He told me what I was doing was against the law, and asked if I was planning to move out of town. I told him I had no such plans. He nodded. Then he took out a roll of hundred dollar bills. He peeled three of them off the roll and handed the bills to me. 'I pay in advance,' he said."

Madam V finished her drink.

"That was the start of it," she said. "Good relations with the cops, you'll pardon the expression, we all understood each other. But not anymore. We have to walk a thin line, dear, and so we keep mum on your Pinky."

"I want to know who he was," Keely said.

"Why? It doesn't matter."

"I suppose not," Keely said. "Maybe I just ..."

"Feel sorry for him?"

Keely shrugged.

Madam V leaned toward her, her cache of neck jewelry jangling. She put her hand on Keely's leg. "That's your natural human goodness expressing itself."

"I suppose."

"Keep that under control," Madam V said. "It can rip you up if you don't watch out. Shall I have another?" She held up her glass. A coating of red V-8 fogged it. "No, too much work to do. Let's go over to the computer and see if we can't figure out who this Mr. Pinky was."

CHAPTER SIX

"I WANT TO KNOW where he is," Ali Botros said. "I want him here. Now."

"May be hard to do," Tim McGinnis said. Normally he would not have made such a remark to Ali, but after an all-nighter with no sleep, he figured he had the right to nudge back They were in the lounge of Ali's yacht, *The Dushara,* a mile off the Malibu shoreline. Tim was seated. Ali hovered over him, bent slightly at the waist, like a curved vine of a Venus fly trap. Botros gripped Tim's lower jaw with his right hand and squeezed.

"Look at my face," Ali Botros said. "Do you see it?"

Tim muffled a *Yes*.

"Do I look like I care if it's hard?"

Before Tim could speak Ali Botros turned Tim's head in a back-and-forth motion. Tim had seen Ali do that before, once, but it was to an unpaid intern.

Never to a partner.

And if he wasn't scared of Ali Botros, he might have protested instead of acquiescing.

Yet he would never have made it physical. No way. Ali was thirty-two and ripped and into MMA. Tim was the same age, creamy-skinned, and slight. He did his grappling with his mind, which is why Ali hired him in the first place.

"You get it done, eh?" Ali said.

"Sure," Tim said.

Ali took his hand away, smiled. Then cuffed Tim with a playful right to the chin. To Tim it almost crossed the border from playful to warning.

"Maybe he lost his phone or something simple," Tim said, rubbing his jaw.

Ali said. "I never should have given that fat pig the time of day."

"He did put up the money," Tim said.

"You can't trust people like that, fifty-year-old guys. Maybe time to reconsider his position. Maybe it's time to get rid of him."

Tim swallowed.

"What's wrong?" Ali asked.

"Maybe we better cool it on that."

"You told me the guy you use is flawless."

"He is, but you can't just keep getting rid of people."

Ali Botros again got in Tim's face.

"Why," he said, "not?"

Tim had the rational thought that killing people you didn't like might get to be a little dicey after awhile. But he said nothing to Ali Botros, who had killing in his bloodline. The public only knew him as a Harvard-educated MBA software star. Tim McGinnis knew the other part, about Ali's father in Saudi Arabia and the international arms deals. Especially the one involving selling Turkey a new and more virulent form of mustard gas for possible use against the *Yekîneyên Parastina Gel*—the Kurdish opposition forces seeking sovereignty just outside Turkey's border.

Because Tim was the information guy, he knew this. He knew, too, that he should never utter a word about it. And also that he should keep it in mind if he ever needed to get out of this devil's bargain he was making and go into witness protection.

Just as Tim was about to break out in hives, Ali shape-shifted back to his other self, the one Tim had seen charm the pants off politicians and prostitutes alike.

"No worries, my friend," Ali Botros said. He went over to the sofa and took up the scimitar that he'd placed there earlier. He sat and placed the sword on his lap. Tim always thought of a child's security blanket when he saw Ali do this.

Ali said, "But when I call for someone to check in at a certain time, I expect him to do it. I expect him to answer his phone. Why hasn't he?"

"Who knows?" Tim said. "Maybe there's an explanation. Maybe he lost it."

"Exactly my point," Ali said, touching his thumb to the curved blade of the scimitar. "Not trustworthy. I should have known. I should have listened to my inner voice. Stupid to trust a man with a nickname like that, what was it again?"

"Pinky," Tim said.

"THE MONEY CAME FROM A SECURE SOURCE," Madam V said, looking at the computer screen. "Can't trace anything that way."

Keely was sitting next to her in the home office. It was a converted bedroom off the dining area, the window facing the narrow beach street. On the screen she saw the record for the client "Pinky." The last payment was $5,000.

"That's all I've got, I'm afraid," Madam V said. "If they don't want to be known, they don't have to be."

"It was worth a shot," Keely said.

"I wish I was better at this," Madam V said. "It was so much simpler when they left the money on the nightstand."

"It's all right."

Madam V shook her head. "I hate all this technology! Apps this and apps that! You know there's someone who wants to take over the whole industry with an app?"

"What industry?" Keely said.

"Our industry! Us! The personal touch!"

"What are you talking about?"

Madam V got up and waved at Keely to follow her. They ended up back at the bar. The nearly empty bottle of Stoli ended up in Madam V's hand. She poured what was left into a fresh glass.

"Starr," Madam V said, pouring the V-8. "She told me about it."

Starr was another of the V girls, same age as Keely. Talkative and lively, Starr was one of those life-of-the-party escorts who appealed to men who wanted conversation before conquest.

"Told you about what?" Keely said.

"Oh this idea that our profession will become like Ebert."

"Like who?"

"Not, who. *What.* You know, that car ride company."

"You mean Uber?"

"That's the one!" Madam V took a swig.

"There's an app for us?"

"It's all very secretive," Madam V said. "Starr said she heard about it from a john who wanted to recruit her. She thought it was all horseradish. But she said she was going to play James Bond."

"What?"

"Go undercover," Madam V said. "In fact, last night. I think she was going to hook up with a guy at that place downtown, what's it called? The Light Bulb or something."

"Light Bulb?"

"You know ... no, wait. I'm getting a little foggy here. The guy who invented the light bulb."

"Edison?"

"That's it! The Edison club. She was going to meet some guy who worked for the guy who was trying to get her to leave me."

Madam V took a long, slow drink, sadness surrounding her eyes. She put the glass down and rubbed the bridge of her nose.

"No loyalty anymore," Madam V said. "Whatever happened to loyalty?"

Keely thought of Traci then.

Madam V took Keely's hand in hers. "You wouldn't leave me, would you? Your Madam V?"

CHAPTER SEVEN

A WOMAN ANSWERED. "CMA."

"I want to speak to the agent who handles Jimmy Hansen," Keely said.

"One moment please."

Another woman's voice. "Mr. Bullock's office."

"I'd like to speak to Mr. Bullock, please."

"Mr. Bullock is not in. May I take a message?"

"Where is he?"

"Excuse me. What is this in regard to?"

"This is a police matter."

"Are you with the police?"

"Would I be calling you if I wasn't?"

"Can you identify yourself, please?"

"Detective Muriel Rodriguez."

"Is there a number where you can be reached?"

"I'm not buying into that. You tell me where he is now. One of his assets is in real trouble and he needs to know about it."

"Oh my gosh, has something happened to—"

"Yes, something has happened to Jimmy. And if he wants to handle it without a lot of noise I need to get in touch with him."

"I'm not allowed to give out his number, but I can contact him and have him contact you."

"Tell me where he is."

"I can't do that."

"Shall I come down there and take you in as a material witness or something?"

"You can't do that."

"Let's play chicken. It'll take me fifteen min—"

"He's actually with Mr. Hansen, I mean ..."

"With him?"

"The football team is practicing. And he doesn't like to be disturbed when there's practice."

"Oh, well, we certainly don't want him feeling disturbed, now do we?"

"I—"

Keely hung up.

THE UCLA CAMPUS in Westwood was a sprawling affair. Almost a town unto itself. The good thing was that Keely knew it well, having been on the payroll of a certain professor of history who had a fantasy about bedding students but was smart enough to know that any such pursuit in reality would cost him his job. He made Keely wear a UCLA sweatshirt.

The team was practicing on the intramural field near the John Wooden Center. A smattering of students watched from outside the fences. Keely made Tad Bullock in a second. He was inside at about the fifty yard line, sitting on a bench. He was as un-student-like as one could possibly be. He did not wear loose clothes or have a backpack at his feet. He was dressed in a black form-fitting suit, wore wraparound shades under thick black moussed hair. He was looking at his phone and tapping away.

Keely went in and walked along the blue track and sat next to him.

He said, without looking up, "If you're a detective, I'm Justin Bieber."

Keely said, "You're better looking onstage, Justin."

Now he turned his sunglasses her way. His head moved up and down as if he were examining a Ferrari.

"I've seen it all, but never in such a great package," he said. "Congratulations."

"For what?"

"For making it past the gate. You know how many girls want to meet Jimmy?"

"I don't really care."

"You can drop the hard act," he said. "I'm on your side. I'm going to introduce you. It takes real cashews to do what you did. You know what can happen to somebody who impersonates a cop?"

"Is it worse than what happens to a first-round prospect who beats up women?"

Tad Bullock paused, then pulled his sunglasses off. His eyes were the color of a Bel-Air swimming pool.

"You disappoint me," he said. "You're a reporter."

"I'm not here to talk about me. I'm here to give you a warning."

He smiled like someone who'd been threatened before and liked to bounce those threats off his teeth.

"How about having a drink with me?" he said.

Keely snorted. Not her best sound, but it fit.

"We can have a friendlier talk," he said, laying emphasis on the *friendlier*.

The guy had a major case of MPD—Magnetic Power Delusion. How many times had she seen it in her professional life? She wished she could bottle it and sell it to inflated egomaniacs like this guy. It would be like a drug. They'd keep coming back for more.

Keely looked out at the field. The players all wore bright white practice pants. Some of the players had blue jerseys, the others yellow. Their helmets were gold.

"See number twelve?" Bullock said.

Keely didn't answer.

"He's in shotgun now," he said. "Watch the magic."

The center hiked the ball to the quarterback who took a few steps back, looked downfield, and fired a strike to a receiver just inside the right sideline. The ball had no wobble at all.

"See what I mean?" Tad Bullock said. "That is what we are talking about. That is a once-in-a-generation asset. I'm talking Elway. I'm talking Wentz."

"Are you ready to kiss your asset goodbye?"

"Now look. Jimmy has cleaned up his act. There's no secret about that. He's like any other college kid. You get rowdy. Things happen. And when you're as good as he is it's very easy for people to lie about you."

"You like to make deals. That's what you do, am I right?"

"Sure. And I'd love to deal with you."

"Then here's the deal. And by the way, it's non-negotiable. Jimmy's been running around with a friend of mine. Her name is Traci. She's in the hospital right now. Did Jimmy tell you about that?"

"You trying to say that Jimmy was involved?"

"I am saying it. There is no try."

"That's another one that's not going to work. You know how many people tried to extort him? You know what the penalty for that is? A lot worse than pretending you're a cop."

"You don't even know the facts."

"I don't have to know the facts."

"I'm going to give them to you," Keely said. "You talk to Jimmy after practice. You tell him about Traci. And then you tell him he's not to contact her, call her, drive by her place, look at her picture online, or think about her in the privacy of his own bathroom. Because if he does, I'm going to bring him down. And I will do everything I can to drag you down with him."

"Who are you?"

"I'm somebody with nothing to lose, but who gets great pleasure in scraping scum off this city's shoes. Your Jimmy will try to deny what he did. You will look into his eyes and you will know that he is lying. Then you will deliver my message. And just remember all those millions you're dreaming about. I hope you dream about a wad of Benjamins in your throat as you choke to death. When you wake up in a cold sweat, you can think about me."

He glared hard for a moment, then smiled. His teeth were as white as bleached bones. "Bravo. That was terrific. Who are you, really?"

"Good-bye."

"Wait, I mean it. How would you like to work for me?"

Keely couldn't help another snort.

"What's so funny?" Tad Bullock said.

"Just a story my grandma told me," she said. "About the frog and the scorpion."

Tad kept his smile. His teeth glistened in the sun. "Tell me."

"A scorpion wants to get across a river, but can't see how. He bumps into a frog and asks him to take him across on his back. But the frog says the scorpion might sting him and kill him. But the scorpion says no, I won't, because if I do we both drown. See?"

"Some story. Sounds a little like my business."

"So off they go. In the middle of the river the scorpion stings the frog. The frog goes, Why, why? And the scorpion says, That's my nature. It's what I do. And they both drown."

"Your grandmother told you this?"

"Uh-huh."

"Must have really helped you sleep," he said.

"I never forgot it, for sure. I don't want to be anywhere near you. You'll sting. It's what you do."

He nodded slowly. "I like it. You're absolutely right." He leaned toward her. "You come in with me and I could teach you how to sting."

"Not if you've got Jimmy Hansen in your stable. I couldn't stand the smell."

Tad Bullock sat up straight. He put his sunglasses on. "Message received," he said.

Keely stood.

"Just one thing," Bullock said.

Keely waited.

"This town's a pretty deep river," he said. "Better be able to swim."

CHAPTER EIGHT

SHE MET AMY AT Musso's in Hollywood. Amy loved the ambience there, and the Martinis. Keely could take it or leave it. She'd met a famous-actor trick here once and he bored her to death, then tried to treat her rough in a room at the Roosevelt. Fortunately, he was one of those wimps who try to pass for masculine these days, and she was able to get to her Mace and fry some theatrical face.

Seated in a red leatherette booth, Amy produced Pinky's phone and placed it on the table.

"Nada," she said.

"Couldn't get in?" Keely said.

Amy shook her head. "And if I keep trying it might all get erased. Sorry, kid. Maybe the FBI."

"For what?"

"Right. What are you going to do?"

Keely shrugged. "I'll keep it for awhile, I guess. Put it in my safety deposit box."

"You have a safety deposit box?"

"What forward-thinking call girl doesn't?"

Amy laughed.

A waiter in a red jacket approached with menus and took their drink order. House martinis.

Keely's phone buzzed.

It was a text from Madam V.

"Business or pleasure?" Amy asked.

"With us it's usually both."

"You ever think of stopping?"

"All the time." Keely looked at the text message. And her blood iced.

"What's wrong?" Amy said.

For a moment Keely couldn't speak. She looked at Amy, and through her. Then she was lost in a dark void, and only Amy's hand on hers brought her back, shaking.

Amy said, "What is it, sweetie?"

"One of the girls," Keely said, her voice barely above a whisper.

"Oh no."

"They found her in her car. Downtown. The back of her head ... shot ..."

Amy squeezed Keely's hand.

Keely said, "I was just talking about her today. Her name was Starr."

"Honey," said Amy, "I'm so sorry."

"You know it happens," Keely said, "but you shove it out of your mind. You tell yourself little lies. When am I going to wake up?"

The waiter appeared at that inopportune moment. He placed their martinis before them. He seemed not to care a bit that her heart was on the tablecloth, bleeding.

He said, "Are you ready to—"

"Can we have a moment?" Amy said.

"But of course," the waiter said with a practiced nonchalance.

Keely imbibed a healthy dose of gin and vermouth.

"Let me help," Amy said.

"Do you mind if we don't eat?" Keely said.

"You need to," Amy said. "Even if it's just some bread."

"I don't want bread," Keely said. "I want to be alone."

TO BE ALONE she always went to the movies.

Even when she first lived on the street in Hollywood, collecting $20 tricks on Santa Monica Boulevard, the movies were her one escape, her passion. Get crazy-good loving with Julia Roberts. Get on a bus with Sandra Bullock. Kick some righteous A with Uma Thurman.

All for the price of a ticket.

She loved the old ones, too, and frequented the revival houses that played classics on the big screen. One of those was the Egyptian Theater, right across the street from Musso & Frank. They were having a Hitchcock fest, and tonight was one she'd never seen in a theater, *Vertigo*.

She got a ticket, went in and bought the largest tub of popcorn they had. She asked for extra butter. She grabbed a handful of napkins and took a seat in the back. She put her head back on the seat and closed her eyes and ate a couple of kernels of popcorn. She told herself not to dig in too deeply, because she loved eating during the movie. She was in the terrible habit of chomping half the popcorn before the previews were over.

If only she could watch movies for the rest of her life and have somebody pay the rent in order for her to do that. A small salary with it. *Movie watcher wanted, make your own hours!*

She thought of Starr then, blown away. An occupational hazard, if you wanted to put it in cold, clinical terms. The same could have happened to her, to any one of them. They all knew that. You'd have to be completely dim not to know and accept it, and if you were that stupid Madam V would not have had you on board. She was known for escorts who could actually carry on a conversation.

The movie started. The haunting credits. The famous score by Bernard Herrmann.

Then the chase across the rooftops, and Jimmy Stewart slipping and hanging on, but a cop trying to help him falls to his death!

Wow.

Then the scene where we learn Jimmy has vertigo now, and that an old girlfriend named Midge still loves him.

When the new scene came up the audience started laughing and cheering. Oh yeah! Because there goes Alfred Hitchcock himself right across the screen! Funny guy, always sticking himself in his own films.

Keely was feeling good, and the popcorn was still warm.

And then there she was, Kim Novak, in the scene at the restaurant, Jimmy Stewart is scoping her for a friend. Keely literally lost breath. Up on that big screen was the most beautiful woman Keely had ever seen, and it was an odd, mirror experience, for that's what her first high-end call had said to her. He was a movie producer, and he'd said, "You are a Kim Novak lookalike. You could be a star." At the time she didn't know who Kim Novak was, but she didn't believe him about being a star, because that would mean she had a legit future and at that time in her life she didn't believe it, not for a second.

Yet here in the dark, looking at the big screen image of Kim Novak, there was a strange sensation, like her spirit being taken out of her body for a moment and melded to that perfect beauty on the screen, as if it were another reality entirely, and she could enter it, dreamlike.

Her longing was palpable. She wanted to be there, wherever *there* was, and stay, never come back.

For the next two hours she was in that dream like no other experience she'd had before, even in the recurring nightmares about the fire and the dead men.

When the movie reached the end, the tragic end, it was like a death to her and not just to Kim Novak.

She didn't want the lights to come on. She didn't want to leave.

Then into the Hollywood twilight, the *Vertigo* theme, that haunting music, suffusing her mind.

Or was it a buzzing?

Yes, buzzing, her phone.

Madam V calling.

"You all right, dear?" Madam V said.

"I think so," Keely said.

"Life must go on. Business, too."

"Ah."

"Tomorrow, six o'clock," Madam V said. "His name is Rich. I hope that's also his state of affairs, and that he becomes a repeat customer!"

CHAPTER NINE

KEELY SPENT THE next morning in her apartment, reading *Pride and Prejudice*, trying to get things out of her mind she didn't want there. Then, at three, she began preparing for her call.

It always started with a half-hour bath using Maison Cauliéres bath oil. This time she chose Tourbillon Végétal, her favorite for the scent of rose petals. She let the water cover her to the neck, with only her knees sticking up, two white buoys in a placid, milky sea. She'd set her iPod to play a medley of Keely Smith songs, mixed with some Diana Krall and Stacy Kent. Always put her in the right mood for service.

For her hair, she used Alterna caviar replenishing shampoo. And when she was patted dry she slipped into her plush fleece robe from Victoria's Secret and began phase two, the Marilyn look.

For this purpose, next to the mirror, she had a framed close-up of Marilyn, looking so innocent and sexual at the same time. She found herself comparing Marilyn and Kim Novak. Both had that vulnerable quality that set off the come-hither eyes and lips. It was Keely's look, too, but all facade. There was no innocence left in her. That had all been burned away.

She applied thick mousse to her damp hair, then blew it dry. Her curlers were hot and ready. She used the smallest curlers on the sections closest to her face and the nape of her neck, and the largest for the crown. When they were all in place she went to the kitchen and poured herself half a glass of white wine. There would be no more than that. She did not drink with a john, ever. Those who wanted to ply her with alcohol got a wicked smile and a finger wagging in their faces. That usually drove them mad, and her Diet Coke would be accepted.

When the curlers had cooled, Keely removed them and brushed out roller marks, then used a comb for the right height and shape. Hairspray for the finishing touch, and there she was —Marilyn.

With the TV on, she replayed a recorded episode of the last season of *Downton Abbey* while she applied red polish to her nails, hands and feet. The old English way of life was slipping away. Keely decided she would have been suited to running one of those estates, bending all the men to her relentless will.

At five-fifteen she put on her red-mesh heart thong and red lace brassiere, then the black faux-leather dress. Then black, open-toe stiletto heels.

It was like a knight preparing for battle, or a matador before the bull fight.

Only this was much more dangerous—a woman who could knock your eyes out.

To get to the call, Madam V provided a car. A nice Town Car from the fleet owned by a Serbian named Pavlovic. At five-thirty, one of his drivers buzzed Keely and announced himself. When she got down to the front she saw a huge, black-clad man. He looked like a slice of the dark side of the moon.

"I'm Mikos," he said. He walked her to the black Town Car at the curb, opened the rear passenger door, and she got in.

And as she did, she asked herself, What if I made this my last call?

"YOU'RE KEELY?"

"Richard?"

"Call me Rich. And may I say that I am more than pleased?"

He was trim, wearing a suit and tie as if that were the most natural thing in the world. Even in the dark reds of the Beverly Hills restaurant she could see he had blue eyes that would dance in the light. He was about six-two.

"Shall we?" He motioned with his left hand and Keely couldn't help the wedding-ring glance. He didn't wear one, which wasn't uncommon with married men out for a joy ride. But she didn't see an indentation, either. Ultimately it didn't matter one bit. Business was business.

He said, "You don't mind the place, do you?"

"Of course not," she said. It was his night, his five grand. He could take her to Arby's if he wanted to. But he was not an Arby's kind of guy, that was clear. A maitre d' showed them to a table in the corner by the window that looked out at Wilshire Boulevard and the commuter traffic.

Rich took up the folded black napkin and whipped it open like a cape, placed it in his lap, smiled at her. If he was trying to practice his charm she was prepared to tell him he didn't need to practice, he had it down. She was guessing he was a Wall Street type. They were much better at smooth than Hollywood producers. The movie guys always seemed to think the whole world was watching them.

"What shall we talk about?" Rich said.

"Whatever you like," Keely said.

"I could ask you where you're from, but I have a feeling you wouldn't be completely open with me."

"Probably so."

"You don't like to open up?"

"This is all about you, Rich."

"How about baseball?" he said.

"I like baseball."

"You're gorgeous. Have you ever thought about giving this up?"

All the time. "For what?"

"Marriage?" he said.

"Like in *Pretty Woman?*" Keely said.

"It happens, doesn't it?"

"It's a myth," Keely said.

"It doesn't have to be."

In a small recess behind her abdomen, Keely felt a small snap, a pinprick of heat. It was where the last of her nerves that processed the possibility of happiness had been consigned, long ago. She knew enough to distrust it.

So why was it flaring now? Her only answer, she was weak. She had been making herself strong for years, and all of a sudden there was a crack in the dam.

Why, why? Was it Starr? Was it Pinky's death? Did something just break loose to show her how soft she really was?

"I can think of much more implausible things," Rich said. "Things like high-jumping elephants, or a Hollywood movie star with an actual thought in his head."

"It's better not to live in dreams," Keely said.

"But isn't that what you give guys like me?" he said. "You let us live a dream for a few hours. And that's a very good thing."

"Is it?"

"Of course it is. We all need dreams. Life is pretty tough. For some people it downright stinks. So if we can escape, in a movie, a good book, or with a beautiful woman who asks nothing of a man but to allow her to give him pleasure."

He was poetic, that was for sure. And a nice respite from the sob story guys who wanted you to know just how much their wives or girlfriends didn't understand his needs, wants, desires, or heroic personality.

If this was to be her last call, it would be a high note to go out on.

CHAPTER TEN

ONE HOUR AND A nice conversation later, they were in his car heading to ... wherever he wanted to take her. He was well off for sure, you could smell that in the car. You could see it in his manicured hands and perfect hair. This man could have been a United States Senator or GQ model. His voice was as smooth as an FM jazz station host.

The little flare in her tummy was still going, and she wondered what it would be like to actually have a man love her, truly. But that thought bumped up against the hard and unrelenting memories of the men in her past, and that flame was effectively tamped down.

When they reached downtown via Wilshire, she assumed one of the hotels would be their landing bed—Omni, Biltmore, Bonaventure. She knew them all from front desk to cleaning closet.

But on Grand he turned left and kept on going, past Disney Hall, the Music Center, across Temple and over the freeway into East L.A. This was not territory she was familiar with. This side of town always seemed like another country to her, like Switzerland if you were crossing the border from France, and French was all you really knew. You knew the cafes and the sidewalks and the bistros and bars. But this other place, you had to be on your guard a little because you didn't speak the language.

Where were the hotels in East L.A.?

On a couple of occasions she'd been taken to a cheap motel, the johns wanting to save a little bit after plunking down five large for the night. If they could spend under a hundred on a room, whoop-dee-doo.

"Can't wait to see what you've got in mind," she said as the surroundings got commercial-industrial.

"Nice and quiet is what I like," he said. "With a little bit of living on the edge."

"The edge of what?" she said.

"The edge of the Los Angeles Unified School District."

She'd had several men who didn't like hotel rooms. Some wanted to stay in the car, which was their choice, though it made her feel like her scuffling days on the street. But what was he saying here? A school? What about security guards? Suddenly she felt like handing him a card that said, *We reserve the right to refuse service to anyone.*

It wasn't a school. It was a lot full of yellow school busses, fenced all around. Dim illumination from the streetlights. He parked at the curb and, as far as she could tell, the street was deserted.

"This all right with you?" Rich said.

"I'm all yours," she said. He did have dark tint on his windows. A preference is a preference.

"Good," he said. "Let's talk."

Oh that. Warm up with a little of the verbal nasty. Which script shall I use?

She said, "Oh, baby, this is—"

"Not you," he said, putting up his hand. "Me."

Whatever.

She waited.

"I've really enjoyed myself tonight," he said. "You have a lot going for you. You're more intelligent than you probably realize. I get a sense about you. This isn't what you should be doing. It's not exactly a long-term profession. You're sort of like an NFL running back. You have a few good years, but by thirty you're pretty much through, and hopefully you haven't had too many concussions. You follow?"

Oh no, a real talker. She got those every so often. She'd be their mother confessor and they'd end up too guilty or too nervous to do anything other than flap their gums. So boring. You got problems? We've got a club for that. It's called Everybody, and we meet at the bar.

"Thanks for the advice," she said.

"I haven't gotten to the advice part yet, but I'm going to. Here's the thing. You and I are more alike than you know. We're both professionals, and both very good at our work. Am I right?"

"I don't know how good you are," she said.

"Because you've never seen me work," he said.

"Logic," she said.

"I'm a great lawyer," he said.

"So you told me."

"You don't believe it?"

"Is this getting us anywhere?"

"That's not all I'm talking about, Keely. I also do something else. And I'm even better at it than I am at the law. If that's even possible."

He smiled again. She could barely see his face, but the white teeth were a can't miss.

She waited.

"Aren't you interested?" he said.

"Rich, look. I'm good at one thing, and that's the thing we're not doing. You've paid your fare and you can spend the time however you want. But maybe we should stop pretending about being interested in other things. Why don't we get a nice room and stop talking so much?"

"*Animus donandi.*"

"What?"

"It's a legal term. It signifies the intent to give a gift. I am going to give you a gift."

"I could use a set of tires," she said.

"More than that," he said. "The gift of life."

An evangelical! She'd had one before, he wanted to save her soul. Paid good money so he could share the gospel with her. He was pretty good, too. Used the Gideon Bible right there in the hotel room. She stopped listening after Romans 6. She even got up to leave. The guy asked for a refund and she said she'd send his church a check. She never did.

"Thanks anyway," she said. "But if there's a God he certainly lost interest in me a long time ago."

He laughed then. "You and me both. No, I'm talking about your actual life, your living and breathing life. That's the gift."

Uh-oh.

"That's what I do," he said. "I kill people. And I'm very good at it. The best, in fact."

Sometimes they said things like that, to mess with her.

"I reserve the right to refuse service to anyone," she said. She tried the door.

Locked.

She tried to unlock it, couldn't.

When she looked back at him he was holding a knife.

CHAPTER ELEVEN

"THEY DESERVE WHATEVER THEY get," his father was saying. "A dirty people. A profane people."

Ali's father, Adnan Botros, lifted his glass and smiled. He'd scored another victory in international arms, only this one would be secret. He looked perfectly content sitting in Ali's penthouse apartment in Westwood. Perhaps because he knew he could buy this entire building ten times over if he wanted to. Or perhaps because he was one of the few men Ali had ever known who seemed invulnerable. No weaknesses. No opening for attack.

Which always made Ali feel like he was still eight years old, living in Riyadh, having the lessons of life beaten into him.

"Are you going with the gas?" Ali said.

"A form of it," his father said. He wore a gray suit and black tie, and the thick mustache he'd always favored. When he was a boy, Ali asked his father when he could grow a mustache, too, and his father had said, "When your face has earned it."

Earning things. That was his father's life lesson.

But Ali was a man now and his face had earned the right to tell his father a few things, too.

"The Americans don't like chemical weapons," Ali said.

"Americans are naive. They go around saying that all people

yearn for freedom. What childishness. People don't want to be free. They want power. They want to be taken care of by power. That's what they didn't get about Saddam, who I knew very well. We were having coffee once overlooking the square as five of his Republican guards used rifle butts to kill a man in the street."

"You've told me this story, Baba."

"I asked who they had killed, and he said, 'It does not matter, does it?' And he waved his arm at the crowd below. 'They understand, and they love,' he said. They did not want freedom, that crowd. They wanted Saddam, and when the Americans came in they thought they could turn Iraq into some version of Pennsylvania."

His father seemed to inhabit the memory for a long moment, a little smile on his lips.

Then he returned, and said, "You're doing well, my son?"

"As you can see, Baba."

"It is not just what you own that makes the man. It's who you own."

Ali nodded.

"Any of the local politicians?" his father asked.

"Yes, Baba."

"The mayor perhaps?"

"Not yet," Ali said.

His father nodded. "That is a good word, *yet*. I am proud that you say it."

CHAPTER TWELVE

"DON'T BE AFRAID," RICH said. "I just want to talk."

"I don't need that thing stuck in my face, if you don't mind."

"You don't need it, but I do. You can't possibly understand how wonderful this is for me. You are actually doing me a good turn."

She couldn't take her eyes off the blade. It was at least six inches long. Where had it come from? Maybe under his seat.

He was going to kill her. You don't bring out a knife on a call girl unless you intend to use it. He was going to get off talking to her in that calm way, and then he was going to slice her throat.

Her purse was on the floor, between her feet. Inside she had a keychain with a small can of Mace. She wouldn't be able to get to it.

"You are extremely smart," he said. "That's a fantastic quality in a woman who looks like you. Most of the time looker hookers are airheads, not worth five seconds of my time. But you have a lot to offer, and I want you to keep offering it."

He tapped his chin with the point of the knife.

Instinct. That's all this was, as Keely felt her hand strike out at the butt of the knife. She intended to push the blade into his face. Her only chance.

But it was as if he had been waiting for her to do that. Before her hand made contact he whipped the knife to the side and with his other hand grabbed her wrist. His grip was iron. He pulled her arm down and placed the sharp edge of the knife across her wrist and pressed down slightly.

"I appreciate the effort," he said. "I like initiative. But don't do anything like that again. I want to leave your face unmarked."

What? Could he really mean he didn't intend to kill her? All she could do now was go with the program, whatever it was.

"What's next?" she said.

He released her arm. He held the knife with the blade pointed at her chest.

"The client before me," he said, "was a man I believe you knew as Pinky."

"Who?"

"Now here is where you're starting to act not so smart. I know it and you know it, so don't pretend with me. You are taking away the entire pleasurable exchange we have going here. Don't lie. I can't stand that."

"Haven't you been lying to me all this time?" she said, wondering what the heck she was doing talking back to this guy.

"There is a difference between deception and lying," he said. "But thank you for asking. I went through this whole process in order to get you right here so we can have this exact conversation. Now, good old Pinky had in his possession a phone. That phone has not been recovered. That leads me to believe that you are in possession of it. What I surmise happened is this. Mr. Pinky, who was not the healthiest of men, checked out in his sleep or maybe even while the two of you were conducting your business. That made things a little embarrassing for you. Since you didn't know who this man really was, because who would call himself Pinky? I mean, really? He was trying to hide his real identity. So you took his phone in order to be able to establish his identity should that become necessary to protect you from the police, or perhaps you thought maybe you would notify the next of kin? I haven't really thought that through, so I wanted to ask you, why did you take the phone?"

There was no use lying to him. His assurance was overwhelming, washing over her like a toxic sludge.

"You're right," she said. "That's why I took it. If you want it back, you can have it."

"Where is it now?"

"In a safe place."

"Not specific enough."

"Do you want the phone or not?"

He smiled. "I like how you use the little bit of leverage that you have. It's really exciting. Kiss me."

"What?"

"Are you forgetting that this whole evening belongs to me? I want you to kiss me now, and I want you to make it count."

Her professional skill had taken a flyer. How could she kiss this guy? She was repulsed. Her stomach rebelled. Even though she had done so hundreds of times with lots of other men, she'd never been with someone who held a knife to her.

She closed her eyes and went into a clinch. The moment her lips touched his she felt the sharp tip of the knife at the back of her neck.

His kiss was long and sloppy. For a moment it felt to her like he was losing control. She wondered if he would plunge the knife through her neck anyway.

He didn't.

But he did sigh.

"That was nice," he said. "Now take me to the phone."

"I can't do that," she said.

"And why is that, my dear?"

"It's in a safety deposit box."

"Now that is very inconvenient. But I suppose they have their rules. I have my rules."

"I will give it to you tomorrow, and then we'll be done, right?"

"You will give it to me, yes. I'm not going to let you out of my sight until I get it."

"That's going to make a very long night," she said.

"You bet it is," he said. "And I'm going to put you through your paces."

CHAPTER THIRTEEN

ONCE, BACK IN BISMARCK, when she was ten, there was a boy named Tommy Abbott, her age, and she was sure even then he would grow up to be an ax murderer. One day he rode his bike by her house and stopped when she was picking a flower from her mom's garden. He told her to come and look at something. He had this expression that was mean and disgusting, but also challenging. She did not want to come off as scared, especially to Tommy Abbott, so she went over to him and he opened up a fanny pack. There was a lizard inside. Keely jumped back a little and Tommy laughed.

Then he said not to be a 'fraidy cat, just look at it. She didn't know why she needed a second look, but once again she didn't want him laughing at her the way he did with other kids. She looked in the fanny pack and saw the lizard again. It was about five inches long and she could have sworn it was trembling.

Tommy Abbott took a long piece of string out of his pocket and reached in the fanny pack and grabbed the lizard. He tied the string around the lizard's neck. Then he tossed the lizard on the street and tied the other end of the string to his bike. Keely asked him what he was doing and he told her to shut up and watch.

He started to pedal his bike and the lizard skidded by Keely's feet.

She yelled at Tommy to stop but he just laughed and rode down to the corner. Then he did a u-turn and rode back to her.

She didn't want to look, but knew she had to. The lizard was twitching and there was dark liquid coming out of its stomach.

With Tommy's cackle following her, Keely ran into her house. She went into her room and buried her head in her pillow and cried.

Keely had managed not to think of that lizard for several years, but the morning after with Rich, or whatever his name was, she felt like that lizard.

He had certainly dragged her along.

They were in a motel and she was laid out on the bed. She'd tried once to fight him off, but he was ready and he liked it. He was incredibly strong and seemed able to anticipate not only every action she might take, but every thought she might think.

What was that story her grandmother used to tell her? About the man who wrestled all night with an angel?

She had wrestled the devil, and he'd won.

When she was able to focus she saw that he was making coffee in the cheap coffee maker.

He noticed her looking and said, "It'll be ready in a minute, hon." He was already dressed, as if nothing had happened in the last twelve hours, as if his games and threats and borderline tortures had been nothing more than watching a late-night movie.

"How do you like yours?" he said.

She turned on her side, pulling the covers over her.

"We have some time before the bank opens. Would you like to take a nice drive?"

She tried to think of another way to get away from him, but knew it was futile. The only way she was going to get rid of him was to give him the phone. And then she was going to tell Madam V it was all over. She'd figure something else out.

Sure.

. . .

SHE PUT a reasonable facsimile of a face on herself before they left. He had allowed her to have her purse, but he put her phone in his front pocket.

"We will make a fair exchange at the bank," he said.

And then they were off in his car. He talked the whole time, telling her about some complicated litigation he'd been involved with and how he'd chewed up the other side because he had "the heart of a lion" and most people only have "the heart of a poodle."

Quaint.

He drove moderately, as if he were enjoying her company.

Why not? It was another sunny day in L.A.

He took Sunset, and when they passed Western he said, "I hate to conclude our time together on a business note, but we need to wrap things up. You go in and get the phone and bring it to me, I'll give you your phone back, and you'll never see me again. Though I have to tell you, it wouldn't be unpleasant for me to spend another evening with you."

Keely thought she might vomit.

"Just don't do anything intemperate," he said. "Like trying to alert someone in the bank. Or calling the police. If you do that, our deal is off. You will be in breach. I will then have to do some things that will make further business between us impossible. Tell me you understand."

She nodded.

"Tell me out loud," he said. "This is an oral contract, if you'll pardon the obvious irony."

"You're just hilarious," she said.

"Do you understand our agreement?"

"Just get me to the bank. I have what you want and you're going to get it. Even you can understand that."

. . .

HE PARKED IN THE lot in front of the bank, in a spot where he could watch the front doors.

"Remember," he said, "nothing rash. It's not in your best interest."

"Thank you for telling me what's in my best interest," Keely said.

"I wish I'd met you before all this," he said.

"Let me out," she said.

He smiled and unlocked the doors.

"HELLO," Terry said. She knew it was Terry because his name tag said *Terry*. He wore a black turban and black suit and a plain, Navy blue tie. "How may I help you today?"

"I'd like to get into my safe deposit box, please," Keely said.

"Of course," Terry said. He opened his desk drawer and pulled out a form, placed it in front of her. "If you will just make that out I will have Anya take you in."

Anya was waiting at the glass door and opened it when Terry and Keely approached. Anya took the form, then walked to the safe deposit room and retrieved Keely's box, number 507. She placed it on a raised table with dividers.

"You can tell me when you're finished," Anya said. "I'm right outside."

"Thank you."

Keely unlocked the box and flipped open the top.

Pinky's phone sat there like an intruder next to two stacks of one-hundred-dollar bills. Two thousand dollars in all.

What if she just took the money, left the phone, and tried to run?

Well, no, he had her phone and could do whatever he wanted with the information.

Did she care what he did?

Just give him what he wants and he'll go away.

But what if he doesn't?

The thoughts and calculations just kept on coming, bouncing around in her head like pinballs, but the big light that kept flashing was *No*. It went on and off with bells and alarms sounding.

No!

She wasn't going to let this animal win.

Then the sound stopped and the lights went off, for he held all the cards.

She wished she could crawl into the safe deposit box and pull the lid over herself, and have Anya put her away for safekeeping.

Finally, she asked Anya to bring her a white business envelope. As she waited for it, she put the two grand in her purse.

THE SECURITY GUARD inside the bank was named Cedric. She knew he was named Cedric because that's what his name tag said. She was beginning to think she was a real detective.

"There's a man outside in that Caddie," Keely said. Cedric was black and muscular, about thirty. The perfect age and build for a bouncer or security guard. "I'm supposed to give him something and he's supposed to give me something. But I'm afraid of him."

Cedric scowled. "You need to call the police."

"No," she said. "I would just like you to stand outside by the ATM for a moment, just to watch."

"Ma'am, I'm not supposed to get involved in anything like that."

"Cedric, I'm too young to be called ma'am. All I want you to do is stand there for two minutes until this is wrapped up."

"I don't know ..."

"I'll forgive you for calling me ma'am if you do."

WHEN SHE WAS ten feet from the Caddie Rich got out, stood there, shades and all, smiling.

"There's something about you I just don't trust," he said. "But if you hand me the phone, I'll reassess."

"Not gonna happen," Keely said.

She watched his cheeks tighten and felt good about that.

"You see that guard there?" she said. "He's watching. Here's how it's going to go down. You are going to give me my phone first. You see, I really don't trust you, either. I think you might not even have it."

"You're starting to deviate," he said.

"Hand it over."

"I could drive away right now."

"You won't. I have what you want. And after last night you're not going to get it, you're never going to get it, until you hand me my phone first. Take it or leave it."

The smile came back. "I'm really liking you more and more. You sure there isn't some way we could turn this into an ongoing thing? You and me?"

"Before I throw up on your shoes, give me my phone."

"You realize I can find you whenever I want to, right?"

Keely said nothing.

"You realize that I will not be as charming if there has to be a next time, right?"

"Be still my heart," Keely said.

Rich reached into his front pocket and pulled out her phone. He held it in his left palm and put out his right hand.

Keely, with reflexes that surprised and pleased her, snatched the phone away.

Rich made a move toward her, looked past her, and stopped.

"Trust me," she said. She opened her purse and dropped her phone in. She pulled out the envelope and handed it to him.

"Bye, sweets," she said, and walked back toward the bank and Cedric the Security Guard.

She walked fast.

CHAPTER FOURTEEN

LARRY WHITNEY—WHO used the name "Rich" when he was out among them—did want to see her again. There was something about her, a raw, undeveloped spirit, and it was vibrating his bones in a way he had not experienced in a long, long time. Not since that first kill when he was still a law student at Stanford. Her name was Tippi, it really was. Her mother had named her that because she loved Tippi Hedren in *The Birds* and *Marnie,* two Alfred Hitchcock movies of the '60s. And this law student did look a little like her, blonde and icy and intelligent. She was rumored to be sleeping with a guy on the swim team, and Larry found he could not resist the challenge.

He started his charm offensive one day in the quad when Tippi was eating a sack lunch with another female student. For two weeks, in addition to studying the laws of jurisdiction, he'd been reading and underlining a copy of *The Will to Power.* Now he was ready to test it all—his power and his jurisdiction over the female sex.

It worked, and Tippi met him at a Mexican restaurant for dinner where they had margaritas and fajitas. Then it was back to her place in Palo Alto. She wanted him, and when he knew he was going to kill her the *kraft* and *macht* coalesced in his spirit in a way that almost knocked him out with ecstasy.

After he'd strangled her he planted the DNA of the swimmer, which he'd procured from his locker, and spread it around and on a knife from the kitchen. He used the knife post-mortem on Tippi, then slipped out into the night.

His proudest moment was showing up in Criminal Procedure the very next day and answering the professor's question about whether police needed a warrant to enter a suspected crime scene. "Only if there is an exceptional circumstance," Larry had answered, "such as hot pursuit or evanescent evidence or consent. If the scene is only *suspected* of being a place of criminal activity, a judge or magistrate must approve a search warrant based upon probable cause."

The other students had looked at him in awe and wonder. If only they knew.

The swimmer was arrested for murder. He had shown up at Tippi's apartment a little after eleven, just as Larry had arranged via an anonymous phone call. The swimmer tried to sell that story but the jury did not believe him.

He was now serving twenty-five to life in Vacaville.

Sitting now in the bank parking lot, admiring the back side of Keely Delmonico, Larry wondered if he could stop himself from finding her again.

Yes, he'd agreed to leave her alone.

But you could consider that just an opening negotiating position.

With a sigh he tore the envelope open and shook the phone out onto his hand.

Only it wasn't a phone.

It was a compact mirror.

He looked at the bank.

Keely and the security guard were gone.

CHAPTER FIFTEEN

"THE COPS," CEDRIC SAID. "You should go to the cops."

No, no cops. She tried that before, tried that with her stepfather and uncle, both ex-cops themselves, and they didn't do a thing, the cops back home. They said she was making it all up.

That did it for her faith in cops.

"Just get me out," Keely said.

Cedric showed her the side door. Outside was an AutoLads store just across an asphalt strip.

That's where she ran. She wasn't going to go anywhere on foot so long as *he* was out there.

AutoLads smelled of cleaning fluid and oil. Keely had been in here only once before, to buy some Tic-Tacs. The cashier had laughed at her, asking her if that was all she wanted, and Keely said that she knew as much about cars as a squirrel did about books. But she remembered the place had a section where only the workers could go, with high shelves and stacks of car parts.

That's where she headed, fast.

Just inside the doors she pulled her phone and got paranoid. Maybe the guy was tracking her. She didn't know about the technical stuff regarding phones and GPS, except that there were ways to clone a phone by putting up another one against it.

Tin foil. You could make hats out of tin foil to keep aliens from taking your brain waves. And keep people from tracking your GPS.

She found a skinny guy in an AutoLads shirt, with red frizzy hair. He smiled and asked if he could help her find anything.

"Do you have any tin foil you can spare?" she asked.

"Spare?"

"Yep."

"Um, I don't, but on aisle nine, we have—"

"I just need a square."

"Is something wrong?" he said.

"Yes."

"Well, maybe in the back."

"You have a room in the back, employees only or something?"

"Um, yeah."

"Will you take me there?"

His facial expression told her that he misunderstood completely.

"And I'm not crazy," she said. "But time's wasting." She put her hand on his shoulder. "Please do this for me, I won't be long."

He thought about it, looked around as if seeking the eyes of his boss, then said, "Follow me."

He took her past boxes of spark plugs and batteries and brake pads, into a small back room with two severe-looking chairs and a metal desk. There was a phone on the desk, a landline, and the place was not exactly a picture of organization. Papers spilled out of an inbox, pink and yellow and white. A half-empty (or half-full, she reminded herself) Starbucks cup sat on the corner of the desk.

And on a crowded credenza was an open take-out box with a lovely square of tin foil inside.

Keely shut the door.

"Hey, wait," Red Hair said.

"There's a man who wants to hurt me," Keely said. As she spoke she took the tin foil out of the box and shook off a few crumbs, and wrapped it around her phone. "He's not my boyfriend, he's a stranger. But he's been following me. All I want is to call a friend and have somebody check to make sure the guy isn't in the store. Will you do that much for me?"

"Only if you buy some wiper blades," he said.

Comedian.

"That's cute. but really, this isn't funny. Would you just see if there's a man out there, about six one or two, black hair, white long-sleeve shirt, dark blue slacks. Might be wearing shades. Can you scope it out without being noticed and come and tell me if he's out there?"

CHAPTER SIXTEEN

LARRY WHITNEY PICKED UP the plastic spray bottle of Armor All but didn't look at it. He scanned the store, picking out people and scoping out places where she could be crouching. He would find her. He would get what he wanted. He always did. Later, he would take care of the rest. She would die the way he liked it.

He began to walk outside the aisles, searching. In his mind he went through scenarios, from her screaming rape to her trying to run, and clicking off answers for each.

Most likely he would find her cowering and quiet, and he would use his powers of advocacy, of convincing her that she had just put her closest friends and family in jeopardy. He would make it abundantly clear that he could find any of them, and that this foolish attempt to deny him the phone was costing her more than it was worth. He'd be softly persuasive.

If she didn't have the phone on her things would be a little more complicated, but only a little.

He liked it. Complications made the challenge greater, and the arousal was worth it.

One more wrinkle, though. What if she wasn't in here? He figured it was the only place she could disappear in, though there was a Baja Fresh and Starbucks across the street. But she wouldn't have been that fast.

Still, she was resilient, this one. She was going to be in his hall of fame.

When he got to the end of the aisles, he turned and looked back and saw a kid with red frizzy hair looking at him. The moment they made eye contact the kid looked away.

"Excuse me," Larry said.

The kid pretended not to hear him.

"I'm talking to you," Larry said.

The kid turned around. His face was a neon sign flashing SHE'S HERE!

"Can I help you find something?" the kid said.

Larry almost laughed. "You sure can. My wife ran in here, and she needs her meds."

The kid's Adam's Apple bobbed up and down. It seemed like it was the size of a ping pong ball.

"I just work here," he said.

"You know what'll happen if she doesn't get her meds? She's sick. She's not well. I love her, but she does this all the time. Now please, help me. Is she in the back there somewhere?"

The kid's chest started moving, the breaths rapid.

"She probably told you to hide her," Larry said. "Like I'm dangerous or something. Listen, kid, she's NOT WELL. She suffers from paranoia and has been in and out of hospitals. We were just at the bank and she ran out of the car."

The kid didn't say a thing. His eyes twitched.

"If you don't help me, you could subject yourself and this store to massive liability. I'm a lawyer. I don't want to threaten anyone, but I do want my wife. She needs me right now. You understand?"

The kid nodded slowly.

"Good. Then take me to her. Now."

The kid's eyelids went up and down a couple of times. Then he nodded and turned.

Larry followed him.

As he did he could not help thinking of the dismal state of the young these days. Weak, wimpy, no will to power, no heft. No wonder America was in the shape it was in. It was raising up generations of participation trophy getters. No one was learning how to take by force. They all ended up working in places like this, or McDonald's or Foot Locker. They will be eaten up eventually.

Then he thought of Keely Delmonico, soon to be dead. She had a will to power in her. He could always tell. He almost thought he should let her live just so the strong side should carry on and perhaps procreate. What if he had a baby with her?

He smiled at his own fertile imagination.

They were in the middle of a valley of shelves now, walking between the automotive parts mountain range.

Then the avalanche came.

A load of heavy boxes fell on Larry Whitney's head, and just before he blacked out under the contents of a falling shelf, he thought, *She did this.*

CHAPTER SEVENTEEN

People started streaming towards the sound of the crash. It was perfect timing, and Keely was pleased with herself in a panicked sort of way. She also knew she had to get out of there fast.

As if it were a small chicken sandwich, she unwrapped her phone from the foil. Continuing toward the street she thumbed to her Uber app.

She wasn't near a cross-walk, and didn't care to be. She headed across the street even though there were oncoming cars both ways. She got some honks, a set of screeching tires, and one invitation to join a guy in his truck.

Ducking into the small convenience store at the Arco station, she completed the Uber transaction and got an estimate of five minutes.

She wrapped the phone up again.

"Help you?" The Hispanic woman at the cash register eyed her warily.

"May I wait here just a moment?" Keely said.

"Oh," the woman said.

"I'll make it worth your while," Keely said. "You have Tic-Tacs?"

Uber, God bless it, was right on time. The driver was a young man with thick, curly hair, wearing a floral print shirt and shorts.

He was chatty on the drive. An actor. What a shock. Had an audition for a soap coming up.

As they pulled up to her place he asked her if she would go out to dinner sometime. Keely said she would, just not with him. And good luck getting that soap.

She ran upstairs to her apartment. Inside she changed into comfy clothes, and packed a bag.

Then she took the stairs back down and went into the parking garage. She opened the trunk of her Elantra and threw the bag in, slammed it and went to the driver's door.

Just as she placed her hand on the handle a voice behind her said, "Hold it."

Turning, she saw a clean-cut face on a well-muscled body.

"I want to have a talk," he said.

From the look on his face, it wasn't any kind of talk she wanted. That's why he was down here in the garage.

"Sorry," Keely said and started to open the car door.

The guy slammed it shut.

From her time on the street Keely knew three good self-defense moves. There was the classic knee to the onions. Then there was the fingernail to the eyeball. Finally, depending on circumstances, there was the stiletto heel to the foot, followed by kicking off the shoes and running like mad.

She realized she was wearing Sketchers.

"Who are you?" she said, getting her knee ready.

"I just want to talk to you," he said.

"No thanks."

"You're making trouble for me and I don't like it."

She processed that, and his look, and his age, and the gears clicked in her mind.

"You're kidding me," she said. "Jimmy Hansen?"

He smiled. It was all perfect white teeth and dazzle.

"I'm not a bad guy," he said.

"You beat up women," Keely said.

"I don't. You don't know what happened."

"Wait a second," she said. "Aren't you some hot stuff quarterback?"

"That's what they say," he said, as if it were the most firmly established truth in the universe.

"Then what are you doing stalking me in a garage?"

"Like I said—"

"There's a creep factor here."

"I'm just a normal guy."

"Why didn't you send your agent?"

"He doesn't want me talking to you. I'm doing this as a favor."

"Not interested," she said. "Now back off."

"Look, nobody's gonna believe anything you say," he said. "I thought we could work this out."

"Nothing to work out. I know what you did."

"She fell down some stairs," Jimmy Hansen said. "I wasn't even there."

"Back. Off."

"Okay, okay," he said. "I just wanted to give you a chance, that's all. I really care about Traci."

She opened the door. Jimmy didn't move. She had to squeeze in.

He pulled the door open wide.

"Hey!" she said.

"Nobody's going to believe anything you say. You're a whore. So don't make me any trouble."

He put out his hand and flicked her cheek with his middle finger. A bee sting.

With a final grin he slammed the door shut.

She started the car and squealed in reverse out of her space. She briefly considered trying to run him down, end his career.

But she decided she didn't want to stain her car.

. . .

Lights were exploding behind Larry Whitney's eyes.

A voice said, "Hey, partner, just take it easy there."

Oh no, not easy. Not now. She did it. Nobody's done that to me, ever. She's dead, but I'll enjoy it even more now.

"Just stay there and we'll take care of everything." The voice belonged to a fuzzy brown man. Larry's eyes were not focusing yet.

"Is he going to be all right?" That was another voice. A man in a red shirt. Yes, red, the store colors. He was in AutoLads.

"We'll take care of him from here," the fuzzy man said. Paramedic?

"Shut up," Larry said, and willed himself to a sitting position.

"No, no, partner, not yet."

"Get away from me," Larry Whitney said.

"Easy now."

"It wasn't our fault," the store guy said. "Somebody did this."

With his left hand Larry pushed the paramedic's chest and tried to stand. Pain explosions went off all over his body, like land mines under his skin. He ignored the pain. Just like when he used to burn his arm as a kid.

The paramedic said, "I can't let you go."

"If he feels he can go," the store guy said, "we have no objection."

"Shut up, both of you." Larry's head was the main thing, the throbbing thing, the thing that felt like it was going to crack open. He started for the front doors, staggering like a drunk.

"Please, sir." The paramedic was behind him. Another one came into the store, saw what was happening, and made a move to stop Larry.

"You touch me and I'll see you in court," Larry said.

"We're going to need you to sign a form," the new paramedic said.

Larry told him he could kiss something, and it wasn't a form.

Then he was outside, limping past the emergency vehicle, a couple of gawkers, then the guys working the auto bays. They were right, of course, the paramedics, he was in no shape, he should be looked at, but it wouldn't be them. He'd get patched up and then he'd be about his business.

There was an upside. He was due a couple weeks off at the firm. He'd finished most of the pre-trial work on the Lavely case. Goodman could handle things for two weeks. And with the Labor Day weekend coming up, everything was going to be slow anyway.

Two weeks to concentrate his mind and do what he did best.

CHAPTER EIGHTEEN

KEELY HIT THE 15 FREEWAY, heading toward Vegas. She'd made the drive many times before. Surely Vegas would be a good place to hole up, especially in her profession.

Former profession.

Wait a minute. Ynez Ibarra. She'd gotten out and was supposed to be living somewhere near the world's most famous gambling town. Maybe she could track her down.

One hour went by, and listening to the radio—her tin-foiled phone was still in her purse—was comforting. No thoughts. Just listen to the music. An oldies station, and then country.

She started getting hungry. What fine cuisine would it be?

Then she saw one of those blue freeway signs with the food places on it. There was a DQ. That was the ticket. She used to love going to Dairy Queen with Noona, her grandmother. A DQ sign was always a magnet drawing her back to the few good years she'd had on earth, her Noona times.

Which was what she needed now. If only she could pull some sort of time travel trick and go back and stay forever at an eternal Dairy Queen.

She went in and bought a cheeseburger and fries and a Diet Coke. Then she drove down the block looking for a shady place to eat and listen to the radio. She came to a little park and decided to pull in.

She drove to the far end of the lot and stopped. She took out a napkin and laid it across her lap, then carefully opened the paper around the cheeseburger and bunched it up underneath so it wouldn't drip. She found a local station playing jazz.

And she took a breath. It was like it was the first breath in a day.

She gave herself permission to relax.

There was a play area for children several yards away from her. It had swings and bridges and plastic slides and one long tube for kids to crawl through. There were three large umbrella shaped awnings protecting kids from the sun.

She didn't see a single, upright monkey bar, the kind they had in that park in North Dakota. Keely loved to hop on it and tell Noona, "Look at me! I'm the queen monkey!" Then she'd fall backward, letting the crooks of her knees catch the bar and leave her swinging there, upside down. And Noona would laugh.

Keely heard a squeal of laughter as she popped a fry in her mouth. A boy of about ten was putting one of the swings to work, kicking higher and higher and rolling his head back, laughing. Oh to be able to laugh like that again!

She watched and ate. The cheeseburger was more than service-able, but the Diet Coke was a little flat. The gap was bridged by the fries, which tasted like they'd come out fresh from the oil.

She saw a curly-headed boy of about two kicking a mini soccer ball with his dad standing next to him. The dad was tall and athletic, and it looked as if the boy had inherited good genes. He would kick the ball and laugh, then run up and kick it again. His father followed him around as the boy kicked the ball one way then back the other. No doubt training for youth soccer. Good for him.

There was a sidewalk near the parking lot and the father walked toward a car and called to his son to come over. The boy kicked the ball to his dad, a perfect strike, then ran toward him.

But he hit a crack in the sidewalk and fell forward, doing a face plant on the hard surface.

The boy raised his head and Keely saw him crying.

The father picked him up tenderly and placed the boy on his chest with the little head resting on his shoulder. He stroked the boy's back with his hand and whispered tenderly in his ear.

For one long moment Keely watched and then, without warning, started to cry.

TWO AND A HALF HOURS LATER, she got to Vegas. The sight of the buildings made her stomach turn.

She hated this place. She'd been here many times on paid-for trips with gambling johnnys. She'd had her fill of craps and blackjack and poker and Keno. The shows were fun, but there was something artificial about them, as if the entertainers had sold their souls to one hotel or another, and were biding their time until someone came by to collect.

But in a strange way, she felt like this was the place where she'd start over. It was made for her kind of woman, after all. She didn't belong in a Midwestern town. They can smell damaged goods right away, the way they did in Bismarck when her personality changed and she went Goth for a couple of years.

What happened to Keely?

Nobody wanted to know, really.

She took one of the exits toward the glittering towers.

She was not impressed.

On Lewis Avenue she pulled to the curb in the shadow of The Golden Nugget. Ah yes. She'd been here with that executive from Comcast.

She unwrapped her phone and called Madam V.

"Keely, darling, where are you? I've been trying—"

"Listen, I don't want to be on here too long."

"What?"

"I'm in Vegas."

"Vegas! You can't be, I've got two clients—"

"I'm running. Listen to me."

"Running?"

"Listen! Somebody's after me, a killer, the one who killed Starr."

Pause.

"Did you hear me?" Keely said.

"But how?"

"I don't have time to explain it now. I need one thing. I need Ynez's address."

"Ynez?"

"Do you have one?"

"Honey, we need to get the police involved."

"No! They won't do jack. Unless I can prove something."

"Well can you?"

"Not yet," Keely said. "Do you have something for Ynez?"

There was a heavy sigh on the other end. "Hold on." A minute later she came back on the line with an address.

"I'll be in touch," Keely said.

"Come back to me, honey, real soon!"

CHAPTER NINETEEN

THEY WERE NICE HOMES. A big tract of them. Keely had heard Las Vegas was booming, or had boomed, or was going to boom again. Somewhere there was a boom.

Normalcy. That's what it looked like. And she allowed herself a moment to believe that she could blend in and be normal.

But it went away just as quickly. She'd always be damaged goods. Face it. But with some hard work and a new skill or two, who knew?

After all, Ynez Ibarra had managed it, at least judging by her house. It was in a cul-de-sac. Keely pulled up at the curb and cut the engine. The moment she did the desert heat pounded on the roof and the windows. It took about thirty seconds for her Elantra to become a Dutch oven.

She got out and was blasted from both sky and asphalt with a hot double-whammy. The houses were all cut from the same developer handbook—Spanish tile roofs, white or pastel colors to kick the sun back into the sky. A few small green lawns, but mostly gravel outside with sproutings of hardy plant life or cacti. There were palm trees, though, reminding her of L.A. At least here the streets were cleaner.

Ynez's house at least was on the side of the street where the sun wasn't shining directly. Keely headed for the porch by way of the driveway next to a cactus lawn. Green, red, brown, prickly, defiant plants. She liked that. Maybe she'd adopt a nickname— Cactus Keely. Yes, and dress in cowboy hat and sequins and big white boots.

If only she could sing.

There was no response to the doorbell and a knock on the door.

But there was a side gate. Keely was sure Ynez wouldn't care if she took a look around. A gal from the old neighborhood come to visit, that was all.

She opened the gate and listened. If there was a Doberman or a German Shepherd, she would fast reconsider.

But there was only silence.

She was liking the silence.

The back yard was enclosed by a wall, was made up mostly of gravel, with some kind of friendly tree in the middle with a brick circle around the base. There was also a cement porch with a welcome overhang and a couple of chaise lounges.

Perfect.

Keely lay down on one of them and felt a warm breeze. It was like a friendly welcome. A good sign.

She needed a good sign.

In five minutes she was asleep.

"KEELY DELMONICO?"

Keely floated out of an unremembered dream.

"Keely, what on earth?"

Keely blinked a couple of times. "Ynez?"

"How'd you find me?" Ynez said.

Keely sat up, a little groggy. "Madam V had your address."

Ynez laughed. "Good old Madam V! She knows everybody."

Ynez Ibarra was dressed in business casual—black slacks and red blouse open at the neck. Her figure was dynamite, packed in a five-foot-five package with a beautiful Hispanic face on top. Her hair was the color of desert mountains at night. Keely remembered her eyes as being a soft brown, but now they were hidden behind big round shades.

"I hope you don't mind that I just showed up," Keely said.

"No way," Ynez said. "Come in!"

Her house was nicely appointed, with modest but comfy furniture and decorations and framed prints of Broadway shows. Keely remembered Ynez had a great singing voice and used to talk about making it to New York to become a musical star.

She guessed Las Vegas was a close enough second.

Ynez took a bottle of white wine out of the refrigerator, got two wine glasses out of a cupboard, uncorked the wine. She poured them each a glass.

"I'm in real estate now," Ynez said. "What shall we drink to?"

"Escape," Keely said.

"Hear, hear!"

They clinked. And sat in the living room. Ynez had her sunglasses off now and her eyes were indeed brown. And restful.

"You did it," Keely said.

"Did what?"

"Got out."

Ynez nodded. "And now you want to?"

"Why I'm here."

"You can do it," Ynez said. "I didn't know if I could. It was hard when I got here. But look at me now. I'm in business, and I have Lucy."

"Lucy?"

"My daughter."

"No way!"

"Way."

A warmth and a longing merged in Keely's heart. Could it ever be that way for her? Home, business, freedom, daughter? Life, hope, future? It was like she'd drifted into a dream, only someone else's.

"Husband?" Keely said.

Ynez almost snorted wine out her nose.

"Sorry," Keely said.

"No, no. I just ... he was a dancer. A straight dancer in Las Vegas, if you can believe it. He wanted me to have an abortion. I told him no. He said he didn't want anything to do with the baby. I told him good, and if he ever tried I'd cut off his ..."

"Ahem."

"I thought I better talk to him in language he could understand. His original language is ape."

Keely smiled and looked at the wine in her glass. "Do you really think I can start over?"

"Absolutely! I'll walk you through it. I can save you some steps. There's a great small group at my church, too."

"Church?"

"That was part of my recovery. The biggest part, in fact. It happened after I had Lucy. Everything changed." She paused. "You have a place to stay?"

"Not yet."

"That settles it," Ynez said. "You'll stay here with Lucy and me."

"You don't have to."

"I want to."

"Except," Keely said.

"Except what?"

Keely put her wine glass on the coffee table and leaned forward. "There's something you need to know first."

"I'm all ears."

"I'm not exactly here voluntarily," Keely said.

"Huh?"

"Someone is trying to kill me."

CHAPTER TWENTY

TIM MCGINNIS DID NOT like it when Ali had one of his women present for a meeting. Even though they were unerringly loyal he just never felt right talking about things openly with anyone else in the room.

Ali Botros had no such hesitation. He seemed to get off on it.

The woman this time was a knockout beauty. She could have been Miss Venezuela or Brazil. Smooth brown skin and long, silky black hair. She was in a tight black cotton dress and was barefoot, and just as Tim was sitting down she handed Ali a drink of some kind in a Martini glass.

"Can I have Manya fix you one?" Ali said.

"What is it?" Tim said.

"Serrano Margarita."

"What's that?"

"My own recipe. It has some ground-up Serrano pepper in it. Gives it a nice kick. Try one."

"Sure," Tim said.

Ali slapped the woman on her behind. "Fix one for him, babe."

She smiled and sashayed—that was the word Tim thought of— toward the kitchen.

"Now," Ali said, "tell me."

"There was a problem," Tim said.

"We love problems!"

"Sure," Tim said, and wondered why his voice was wavering.

Ali motioned with his hand, inviting explanation.

"Well, she got away from my guy," Tim said. "It's not like him. But he is going to make it right."

Tim felt his pulse hammering his temples.

"My father told me a story once," Ali said. "About IBM. When they first had the Japanese manufacture some parts. They sent instructions that said, We will only accept three defective parts per ten thousand units. When they got the delivery, there was a note attached that said, The three defective parts you ordered are wrapped separately."

Tim blinked.

"Something was lost in translation," Ali said. "But here we don't accept any defective parts. Yes?"

"Of course," Tim said, quickly adding, "not."

The woman came back holding a frosted Martini glass by the stem. She handed it to Tim.

"Thank you," he said.

"Give it a try," Ali said.

Tim lifted the glass to his lips and sipped. The first sensation was icy cold, followed by a hot kick to the back of the throat.

"Wow," Tim said.

"You like it?" Ali said.

"I'm not sure."

"Take another sip."

He did. Same feeling.

"Well?" Ali said.

"It's ... different."

"You don't like it?"

"I'm not saying that."

"I can see it in your face," Ali said. He looked at the woman. "Did you make it right?"

She seemed surprised at that. Her easy smile faded.

"Yes, I think," she said with a slight Hispanic accent.

"Here, let me," Ali said, rising and taking the glass from Tim.

Ali sipped the drink, rolled it around in his mouth like a sommelier.

And then his face changed.

To rage.

He threw the drink in the woman's face.

She yelped in shock.

Ali threw the glass at the wall, where it shattered. "You made it too spicy!"

The woman was wiping her eyes now. "It hurts!"

Tim wanted to help her. But he was frozen in the chair.

Ali looked at him. "You see?" He thumbed toward the woman. "Defective!"

Tim said, "I didn't mean—"

"I won't take it," Ali said, leaning over Tim, looking at him with the fire of the sun.

Silence then, except for the weeping of the woman and the thumping of Tim's heart.

Then Ali stood, his face softening, his smile returning. He went over to the woman and put his hand around her shoulder.

Softly, he said, "Okay, that's enough, that's all right. Huh?"

She put her head on his chest.

"That's right," Ali said. "Now, there's Serrano Martini all over my carpet. You see that?" He pointed at the area around the woman's feet. She looked, blinking, as if trying to focus.

"That's good carpet," Ali said. "So get down on your face and suck it up."

Tim wasn't sure he heard him right. He couldn't be telling her to literally put her mouth on the carpeting, could he?

The woman pulled her face from Ali's chest and looked at him. At this angle Tim could only see her expression. It was the most fear-filled face he'd ever seen.

"Now," Ali said.

Tim watched in horror as the woman lowered herself to the

floor, put her mouth to the fibers of the carpet, and started to inhale.

"Oh man," Tim said, "you don't have to—" He stopped when Ali pointed at him.

"Be," Ali said, "quiet."

The woman continued to suck carpet.

CHAPTER TWENTY-ONE

"YOU WANT TO RUN that by me again?" Ynez said.

"It's complicated," Keely said.

"I guess so!"

She told her all about it, up to and including her escape from AutoLads and getting to Vegas with Pinky's phone.

"I know somebody who's good with computers," Ynez said. "Maybe he can crack the phone."

The front door opened and closed. A girl about eight entered the room. She had lighter skin than her mother but her hair was just as dark, though not as silky. Her face was roundish and her body was what could charitably be called chunky.

"Keely, this is Lucy."

The girl pursed her lips and did not look at Keely.

"Hi," Keely said.

The girl looked at the floor.

"Lucy, can you say hello?" Ynez said.

Without looking up, the girl fairly whispered, "Hello."

"Lucy! That's no way to say it."

The girl was unmoved.

"Lucy!"

"It's all right," Keely said.

"No, it's not. Lucy, what is it?"

She didn't answer. Her hands were balled into fists.

Then she ran from the room.

"Lucy!"

"Maybe it's me," Keely said.

"It's not you," Ynez said.

"I should go."

"No, stay right here."

Ynez followed her daughter.

Okay, family stuff, stuff she would never know anything about, for she would never have children, never bring a child into this world. Poor Lucy.

A few minutes later Ynez came back, holding Lucy by the hand. "Go on," she said.

"Sorry," Lucy said.

Keely couldn't remember the last time someone apologized to her.

"Oh, it's all right," Keely said.

"She got teased by one of her friends," Ynez said.

"She's not my friend!" Lucy said.

"Lucy, stop."

"Teased, huh?" Keely said. "Teasers suck."

Lucy looked at her with interest, as if waiting for—needing to hear—more.

"Yeah," Keely said. "I got teased all the time as a kid, and look at me now."

Oops. Overreach. The model of adult adjustment she was not.

But Lucy looked at her and smiled. The girl's front teeth had a gap between them.

Digital dance-pop came from Ynez's phone. Something familiar. Keely actually wanted Ynez to let it keep going. Yeah, dance around the room and forget everything!

Ynez excused herself to take the call.

Leaving Keely and Lucy looking at each other.

"Are you going to live here?" Lucy said.

"I may stay here awhile, if that's all right."

Lucy nodded.

"Where did you come from?" Lucy said.

"Los Angeles," said Keely.

"Did you do work there?"

"Uh, yes."

"Did you do real estate like my mom?"

"No."

"Did you sell anything?" Lucy said.

"Say," said Keely, "let's talk about something else."

"Like what?"

Anything else. Oh, anything else.

Ynez came back in the room. "I am so sorry, I've got to get a signature from one of my clients. Keely, could I ask you to watch Lucy for about an hour?"

"Watch?"

"Yeah."

"Um, well, if it's okay with Lucy."

The girl, smiling, nodded vigorously.

Ynez kissed Keely's cheek. "It's so great to see you." She picked up her purse and started for the door.

"Ynez, what was that music on your phone?"

"Huh? Oh. Michael Jackson. *Invincible.*"

WHEN THEY WERE ALONE, Keely said, "So what do you like to do?"

Lucy bit her lower lip. "I like puzzles."

"Really? Why puzzles?"

Lucy thought about it. "When I do 'em I don't think about sad things."

"Aw, what have you got to be sad about?"

Lucy shrugged.

"You're too young for that. What do you want to be?"

She shrugged again.

"I'm sure you've thought about it," Keely said.

Lucy thought a moment, then said, "Police, maybe."

"A cop?"

She nodded.

"What makes you want to be a cop?" Keely said.

"Bad people need to be stopped."

"Boy, have you ever got that right."

"There's lots of bad people in Las Vegas."

"Let me tell you, they're all over."

"Mommy has a stalker."

"What?"

"His name's Buddy."

"Your mom has a stalker named Buddy?"

Lucy nodded. "She had to get a straining order."

"Oh, man."

"He needs to be put in jail for a long time," Lucy said.

"Sounds like a plan."

"Or maybe shot."

"Shot dead?"

"If he's trying to hurt mommy, I'd shoot him dead."

Okay, Keely, walk softly and tenderly. You don't want to say something that will encourage this nice little girl to go pick up a hot firearm on the street. Or end up like her, killing two men when she wasn't much older than Lucy.

"Well," Keely said, "maybe you better wait until you're an actual cop before you shoot anybody."

"But what if I was alone and he was trying to kill mommy?"

"Boy, you ask some heavy duty questions. Don't think about all that now, huh?"

"Okay."

Whew.

"Would you ever kill anybody?" Lucy said.

Ack!

"Why don't we do a puzzle together?" Keely said.

"Okay!"

And so they did, in Lucy's room. It was a horse puzzle. A horse in a pasture with blue sky and clouds and a farm house. It could have been North Dakota. It could have been Noona's farm.

What were the chances?

Yes, let's do a horse puzzle and maybe I can will myself into the picture and stay there forever.

CHAPTER TWENTY-TWO

VIRGINIA MILLICENT MAYFAIR curled her toes in the cool evening sand of Venice beach. She loved the sound of the waves, crashing, like the cheering crowd at a Mexican *corrida*. It was in the city of Aguascalientes that she enticed the legendary bullfighter Alejandro Bravo. She was sixteen. He was forty-two. He left his wife and children for her.

He wanted to make "an honest woman" of her.

Why hadn't she married him? What would her life have been like had she followed the bulls with El Bravo?

Probably the same. She would have left him eventually.

Life was like that. There is a wheel of fate and it goes around and even if you try to get off it brings you back, to the same place.

Madam V believed in Fate. She was destined to be here, even this very moment on the beach.

And destined to help Keely Delmonico in her troubles.

The Pinky issue, as she was calling it, had bothered her all day. But not half so much as Keely running out on her. That wasn't like her. Keely was trustworthy. A real professional, as they say. Madam V would not have brought her on otherwise. Nothing but the best for her boutique.

It was trouble, though, big time. She knew that much. If she could help get her out of it then she'd have her back. And could fulfill all the requests that came in for her.

Such was the pleasure business.

With a deep breath of ocean air, Madam V turned and headed home.

At night, it was home, not an office.

She decided on a nightcap—her own version of a Brandy Alexander. She called it Alexander's Sister, substituting crème de menthe for crème de cacao. It went down velvety and smooth, and was a good companion for reading.

When she turned on the lights in the kitchen, though, it wasn't the liquor cabinet that caught her eye.

It was the man sitting at the table, eating.

A sandwich?

Madam V's throat clenched.

"Do you have any mustard?" the man said. He was lean and muscular, wore a red golf shirt without a logo.

"How did you get in here?" she said.

"I let myself in," the man said.

"But how? I—"

"Doesn't matter. I'm here. Thanks for the bread and cheese, but this is really dry. I didn't see any Grey Poupon."

She wasn't going to wait for him to do whatever it was he was here for.

Mr. Smith and Mr. Wesson would settle the matter.

Her gun was in a drawer of the antique roll top desk by the front door. She knew how to use it, too. She went to the range at least twice a year.

Gun in hand, she returned to the kitchen.

"Now," she said, "who are you?"

The man had a mouthful of food. He raised his index finger to have her wait.

The cheek of this guy was too much. And annoying. She thought then she might shoot him just on principle. *Yes, officer, he tried to jump me. I had no choice but to shoot.*

"I will shoot you. Don't think I won't. I won't mind cleaning up your blood."

The man brushed his hands. "I believe you really will."

Madam V pulled the hammer back, clicking it into place, Old West style.

"A .38," the man said. "Nice."

"I may just shoot you and let the police come and sort it all out."

"That's what I would do," he said. "I like the way you think."

He stood up. A cool one he was.

"Now what I'd like from you is simple," the man said. "Just a little information."

"I'm through talking. I'll give you three seconds to get out."

"I like that, too! The old count down! But I'm going to need more than three seconds. Ten minutes should do it."

"Get out! Now!"

He shook his head. "You'll just have to shoot me, babe."

"Last chance."

He took a step toward her.

He smiled.

Another step.

Madam V pulled the trigger.

And heard *clack*.

She pulled the trigger again.

Clack.

Again.

Clack.

The smiling man reached in his pants pocket and came out with a palm full of bullets.

"It works better with these," he said.

If she had been outside herself, Madam V would have thought what she did next was a cliché, but she did it out of instinct, out of survival mode.

She threw the Smith at him, but her softball throwing days

were long gone, and the gun was heavier than she remembered, and the man ducked it.

And then jumped at her.

She tried to turn, to run, to *move*, but he had her by the hair, her head jerking back, and then she was flat on her back and he was on top, his hand on her throat, squeezing.

"You must have been something when you were younger," he said. "Maybe if you lost a few pounds ..."

She wanted to scream but the clamp on her throat was vicious.

"And now you're going to give me what I want," he said.

"TELL ME A STORY," Lucy said.

"Story?" said Keely.

"Mommy always does."

Keely was on the edge of the bed, Lucy tucked in under her *Incredibles* sheets.

"What kind of story?" Keely said.

"Any kind."

Great. Her knowledge of childhood stories was limited, due to her limited childhood. But she did remember her grandmother telling her one.

"Do you know about the ugly duckling?"

Lucy shook her head.

"Do you know what a duckling is?"

"A baby duck?"

"Right. They're kind of like fuzz balls. Not much to them. They swim around, following their mother. All in a row."

"Cool."

"Okay, so there was this duckling, see, and she wasn't very good looking. In fact, she was ugly. Her feathers were all sticking up all over the place."

"I have a friend named Brianna who has hair like that."

"I bet she doesn't have webbed feet, though."

Lucy laughed.

"Okay, so all the other ducklings made fun of this little duck. They teased her all the time and whenever anybody tossed them some cheese they'd eat it before she could."   *

"That sucks."

"Totally sucks. This duckling's uncle and a friend of his, two really ugly ducks, did some bad things ..."

She stopped. No need to embellish.

"Anyway, the ugly duckling got really sad and went away. She wandered into the forest and almost got eaten by an animal."

"What kind of animal?"

"Um, a bear. Or a rhinoceros."

"What did she do?"

"She tried to join a group of swans flying by. Have you ever seen a swan?"

Lucy shook her head.

"They're the most beautiful birds there are. Some are white and some are black, but the white ones are the whitest white and the black ones are the blackest black, and they both have beautiful wings and if you ever see one, you're going to go awww."

"Cool."

"Very cool. But this little duckling couldn't fly fast enough to keep up with the swans. So she had to stay right where she was, in the dark forest."

"With bears and rhinocerouses."

"Exactly. Then winter came. It was so cold! Luckily she found a cave and went in there."

"What did she have to eat?"

"Um, some campers had left some Pop-Tarts there, and what's your favorite food?"

"Pizza."

"Yes, there was a pizza there."

"Was it frozen pizza?"

"Sure, yes, but she sucked on it and that was good enough. So she stayed in there the whole winter. There was a lake outside the cave, and one morning she heard some noise out on the lake. So she went outside and saw a bunch of swans swimming on the lake."

"Were they black swans or white swans?"

"You know what? There were black and white and brown swans."

"Cool!"

"But the ugly duckling was afraid of them, like she was afraid of the bears and rhinos, and she was about to run away when she happened to look at herself in the lake. And guess what?"

"What?"

"She wasn't a duckling anymore. In fact, she wasn't even a duck! She was a beautiful swan!"

"Wow. What color?"

"Definitely brown. A beautiful brown."

Lucy smiled.

"And the other swans said to her, Hey there! Come on and join our flock! And so she did, and they flew away together."

"Where'd they fly?"

Yeah, where? A picture came up in her mind, a vista of a winding river and sunny mountain buttes against a vivid blue sky. A place her grandmother had taken her once, a big park in North Dakota named for Teddy Roosevelt. A place where Keely had felt an escapist joy for once in her life. A place she wanted to stay.

"Well, they flew to a place called Theodore Roosevelt Park. If you ever go there, you might see a brown swan."

"What happened to the ducklings that were mean to her?"

"They grew up and went into dead-end jobs. Some of them developed drinking problems."

"Really?"

"That's life."

"What about the two big ones that did bad things?"

Keely paused. "They were trapped by a hunter and he cooked them and ate them with orange sauce."

"Whoa."

"That's also life. So here's the moral to the story. Don't let anybody put you down. You find your wings someday, and fly wherever you want to. Okay?"

"Okay."

"Now go to sleep."

Lucy put her arms out. Keely bent down. Lucy kissed her cheek and said, "Good night."

"Good night, sweetheart."

CHAPTER TWENTY-THREE

KEELY AWOKE CALLING SOMEONE'S name.

She didn't know who it was and, fully conscious, didn't remember the name, either.

And for a long moment she wasn't sure where she was.

The room in the morning light looked spare but not cold. Had she been drugged? Or drunk? Did someone drag her in here and put her to bed?

She smelled coffee.

Ynez's. That's where she was.

Would Ynez have a cigarette? Las Vegas seemed the perfect place to start smoking again.

She went to the bathroom and sloshed water on her face, looked at herself in the mirror and said, "Hideous."

Ynez had provided a nice soft robe for her. Keely put it on and went out to the kitchen.

"How'd you sleep?" Ynez said. She was already dressed for business, a black suit with fire-engine red blouse. She poured a cup of coffee and handed it to Keely.

"I guess okay," Keely said.

"You want some breakfast?"

"You wouldn't happen to have a cigarette, would you?"

Ynez shook her head. "Gave it up."

"Shoot."

"I run three miles in the morning," she said, like it was an invitation.

"I walk three blocks every other day," Keely said.

Ynez laughed. "How do you like your eggs?"

"Over and done with," Keely said.

And then Ynez was making her breakfast, chatting away, and Keely felt like she'd dropped into someone else's dream. A nice house, clean kitchen, granite countertops, smells like the best breakfast place she'd ever been in. A woman who had taken her in without hesitation, even though trouble was all over her like an odor. Even in a house with a little girl.

Domesticity. That was never the dream of the pros. Once your body was on sale it was like something deep inside you knew you were cutting off that possibility forever. It was like a double mastectomy. You were never going to nurse a child, you were never going to be caressed with love.

But somehow Ynez had made it. And Keely suddenly felt guilty for coming here. What if she spoiled things for Ynez and Lucy? Was bad luck...a time suck...a burden? Ynez was one-of-a-kind. She'd always been that way, even back in L.A. There was a spirit in her that the girls admired. At least Keely had. And she'd been right. Here was the proof.

Keely didn't want to spoil it for her. And so as Ynez served her the eggs, Keely said, "I should probably move along today."

"What?"

"Go get a room or something."

"Forget that noise," Ynez said. "You're staying with us. Lucy has really taken to you."

"I don't know why."

"Because you're you," Ynez said.

"But I can't just eat your food and take up space."

"How would you like to sell real estate?"

"Excuse me?"

"Do what I do. I could teach you."

"You mean be normal?"

"You'll get used to that," Ynez said with a laugh. "I've got the whole day planned. Lucy's at day camp, I'll show you my office and what I do. And there's a guy there who can look at that phone you have."

"Really?"

"He's a computer genius," Ynez said. "The rumor is he used to work for national security. He can probably handle one phone."

YNEZ WORKED AT CONNOR-REILLY REALTY. The office was in a business park by a man-made lake on the other side of which were houses out the wazoo. It was an explosion of suburbia, carved out of the desert.

The first-floor space of Connor-Reilly was made up of a modest reception desk, some cubicles, a couple of regular offices in the far corners, a conference room and a kitchenette. Ynez introduced Keely to the receptionist, a pretty African-American girl named Terry who was in her third year at UNLV.

Then it was back into one of the offices where Ynez presented Ezra Hirsch, the managing partner. He was short and dark with a sell-you-anything smile.

In fact, the whole place vibrated with sell-you-anything smiles, including framed motivational posters. One that made Keely stop was a picture of a guy hanging over a forest by ropes, presumably from the side of a mountain. He also had his mountain bike dangling with him. The caption said: MAKE IT HAPPEN - There Is No Challenge Too Great For Those Who Have The Will And Heart To Make It Happen.

"You like that one?" Ynez said.

"Wonder if this was taken right before the guy fell," Keely said.

"Come on. I want you to meet Jude."

. . .

JUDE ANDREU WAS in his late twenties, had Viking-blond hair cut with bangs and hanging down to his shoulders. He wore glasses and a black T-shirt with a skull with bat wings on the front.

"Casual Friday," Ynez said, as if reading Keely's thoughts.

"Nice to meet you," Keely said.

"Yeah," Jude said. He was seated at a desk in one of the offices. All around him was computer equipment, speakers, monitors, wires, and two KFC boxes, empty.

"While his social skills can be polished," Ynez said, "his computer knowledge is awesome."

"Huh?" Jude said.

"Keely has a challenge for you," Ynez said.

"Yeah?"

Keely took Pinky's phone out of her purse. "I need to get the data off this phone."

"Why?"

"The guy whose phone it is ... was ... is dead. And there's some other people who want the phone back and I don't want to give it to them."

"Cool," Jude said.

"Is that a good enough reason?" Ynez said.

"For me," Jude said. He connected some kind of cord to the phone, and the other end to a port on his computer. After bringing up a screen that was all numbers he picked up the phone again. He handled it like a precious stone, his fingers holding it lightly while his thumbs tapped out a rumba on the phone.

He nodded and smiled. "Uh-huh," he said.

"What is it?" Ynez said.

"This baby has a secure enclave."

"Meaning?"

"It's a cryptographic coprocessor, stores keys in tamper-resistant hardware. See, a secure enclave imposes longer timeouts on its own on passcode guessing attempts. After a certain number of incorrect attempts, boom, erases the keys."

"Keys?" Ynez said.

"Encryption keys. See, that's how you get to the data. No keys, no data." He looked at his computer monitor and scrolled through some alphabet and number soup. "This one has encryption using an iterated key-derivation function."

"In English, please."

"It requires the phone to take a minimum of eighty milliseconds to check a passcode guess."

"Isn't that fast?" Ynez said.

Jude shook his head. "It's a calculation designed to be complex and slow to complete. Passcode strength affects how long a guessing attack would take. For long passcodes, that delay, by itself, might be long enough to make guessing infeasible even with special cracking software. See, like, if the passcode contained eight random lowercase letters, it would take about seven hundred years to guess at this rate."

Keely's heart dropped. Ynez looked at her with an expression that said *Sorry*.

Then Jude put his finger in the air and smiled. "But! Vee haff vays."

He looked like a comedian waiting for a laugh. Keely and Ynez provided only crickets.

Jude cleared his throat. "See, there are avenues, roads, paths you might say, for a security compromise in the phone's secure boot-loading process. If I found one that could be used to evade passcode rate-limiting, then we might be able to jailbreak this thing and run unsigned code."

"I guess you know what you're talking about," Ynez said. "But there's no way I can tell."

"There's one other way," Jude said. "I've sort of been working on this on the side for a long time, a way to physically extract encryption keys from hardware. But it's messy and there's a risk of destroying the keys before they can be read."

Jude put the phone on his desk, leaned back in his chair, laced his hands together and cracked all his knuckles. "So," he said. "Whattaya want me to do?"

CHAPTER TWENTY-FOUR

WHEN HE WAS SEVEN, Larry Whitney's father took him to see *The Silence of the Lambs*. He was over at his dad's for visitation, that's what he called it, and after they had pizza he said let's go see a scary movie.

His dad bought him a tub of popcorn to go with the movie.

Larry didn't understand a lot of what was going on. It was about a girl and she was trying to be some kind of policeman or soldier or something, and then she was going to see a man in a deep, dark dungeon.

When he saw the man standing there he couldn't take his eyes off him. There was something about this man, who was in a glass cage. Larry, age seven, thought he was looking at himself all grown up. And this guy, his name was Lecter, could control people and do things and kill people when he wanted to, and it was so neat.

Larry Whitney would watch *The Silence of the Lambs* dozens of times over the years, on video tape and then on DVD. And he understood it better each time. Hannibal Lecter was smarter than anyone else.

So was Larry.

Lecter was once a respected professional who everybody feared.

Someday, Larry would be that way, too.

Lecter ate people.

Well, Larry drew the line there.

But the first time he killed someone—that law student, Tippi —he got something so much more satisfying than a liver with fava beans and a nice Chianti.

He got a charge like he couldn't believe.

And this Keely Delmonico was going to be the greatest charge ever.

Driving toward Vegas now, passing Zzyzx Road on Highway 15, always the marker he and his college buds would note on their way. It meant you were only about an hour-and-a-half away from the blackjack and poker and craps tables, and the strippers and call girls.

This time, there would be one call girl in particular, the best of all.

CHAPTER TWENTY-FIVE

"IF ANYBODY CAN DO it, he can," Ynez said.

They were driving in Ynez's Jetta, on their way to one of the homes she was selling.

"He certainly seems like one of those genius types," Keely said.

"Definitely."

Keely sighed.

"What's up?" Ynez said.

"I'm just amazed at you," Keely said.

"Me?"

"You've got it all now. You've got a job, you're making good money, you've got a house."

"And Lucy."

"She's so adorable," Keely said. "And smart. And what's this about a stalker?"

Ynez looked at her. "She told you, huh?"

"Matter-of-factly," Keely said.

"I didn't want her to be scared, but she overheard me talking about him. His name's Buddy."

"Is he dangerous?"

"He wants me to think he is," Ynez said. "So I got a restraining order, which doesn't do much. That's why I have Electra Woman."

"Who?"

"Not who." Driving with one hand, Ynez reached in her purse and pulled out what looked like a pink iPhone. "This is Electra Woman. Twenty-five million volts of girl power."

Keely hefted it. "Ever use it?"

"Not yet," Ynez said. "But I'm itching to."

"THIS IS what we call a sharp little property," Ynez said.

Keely knew what she meant. You could tell by looking. No rogue weeds in the yard, no fading paint on the trim. Not even dirt on the Spanish-tile roof.

"It has curb appeal," Ynez said. She parked at that very same curb. They got out and started up the walk to the front door.

Ynez said, "I know how to show property. I'm a show-er. Let me show you the inside."

Ynez entered a code on a box hanging from the front door handle. A drawer popped out with a key inside. Ynez used the key to unlock the door.

"Smell," Ynez said.

Keely took a sniff. A nice scent.

"My own personal potpourri," Ynez said. "Lucy and I made it."

"Nice."

"You have to appeal to all the senses," Ynez said. "If I'm having an open house I'll set out a plate of freshly-baked chocolate chip cookies."

The house was without furnishings, but the carpet looked new and a skylight let in a generous splash of sunshine. There were pretty hardwood floors. The kitchen looked updated and shiny.

"This is kind of cool," Keely said.

"Why don't you buy it?" Ynez said.

"You have half a million you can spare me?"

"Let me talk to my mortgage broker."

"I'm sure I qualify," Keely said. "I can put my body parts up for collateral."

"And they're still very nice parts," Ynez said, "if you don't mind my saying. Seriously, you'll get settled somewhere, why not here?"

"I don't even know how to think that far ahead."

"We can change that. I'll show you how to set goals and go for it. Like that guy in the poster."

"Just before he—"

"He didn't fall!" Ynez laughed, and Keely joined her, and thought how much like a sister Ynez suddenly felt like, even though Keely had never known a sister or brother.

Ynez's phone Michael Jacksoned. "Ah, I have to take this. Have a look around."

It was a nice house, a warm space. Keely wondered if she'd ever fit in such a place. She'd always been in apartments, squeezed in between odd people who somehow became friends—except for Mrs. Papadoukis in the apartment across from Keely's. She was an old, embittered, self-appointed building sheriff, always carrying on about the noise, the trash, the visitors, the "wild sex parties" and pizza smells.

Wouldn't it be nice to have a house to spread out in?

But what would she do with all that space? Cats? Dogs? Maybe an iguana. Keely had always liked iguanas.

The biggest bedroom was in the front corner at the end of the hall. It was done up in pastel cream. There were big mirrors on the closet doors.

Keely stood in front of one of the mirrors and took stock of herself. What could she do with this package that was Keely Delmonico?

She couldn't dance much, or sing like a bird. But maybe, just maybe, she could be normal.

Was it so far-fetched? Maybe she could be actually ordinary. Live in a house, have a closet. And in that closet would be dresses and shoes and blouses and maybe even some hats. She looked good in hats. A little style.

How much space was there in this closet anyway?

She slid the door open. Quite a bit of space, if you—
She jumped back as a scream stuck in her throat.
The man's head was in a pool of blood.

CHAPTER TWENTY-SIX

LARRY WHITNEY DROVE BY the house slowly, giving it a quick scan. He checked the adjoining houses, across the street, getting the lay of the land. The position of the front door, the side gate adjacent. He checked out the other houses on the block, too, drove to the end of the street which ended in a cul-de-sac, turned around and drove back.

Another scan.

He drove around the corner to the street parallel to the one this Ynez chick lived on. He cruised slowly past the house that would be the one directly in back. He checked for side yard entry and exit. He made mental notes, a map really, and pictured his coming and going, his doing and leaving.

The row upon row of nicely appointed homes, which no doubt had its share of nicely appointed people in them—although he knew statistically a small percentage of them would be sociopathic if not psychopathic—angered him suddenly. He got that way sometimes, as if people in the normal world were judging him. What right did they have to do that?

They all believed they were special creations of some sort, either by God or their own selfish existence. But most of them did not know half the ecstasy he did, and if their illusions made them feel superior it ticked him off.

They also had that awful sounding word for it, thought up by egghead PhDs for their DSM, but they had no understanding, no appreciation if you wanted to know the truth. Because that truth was that we are all matter and destined for nothing, so anything done in this life that brought ecstasy, even with dead matter, was just as worthy as going to church or working in a soup kitchen.

If he could determine every single one of the judges in every single house, and he had the time, he wouldn't mind killing them all.

He drove back into the shopping district and found himself a Starbucks. Then went in and ordered himself a Grande Mocha with whip and found a soft chair by the window. He realized he hadn't fully relaxed in weeks. Not only was there the litigation, but the side jobs he was asked to perform. That was really what he called mixing business with pleasure! But it wasn't always relaxing, with the adrenaline flowing and the ecstasy releasing.

He hadn't read a book, other than some legal tome, in a couple of months.

He had the new Harlan Coben on his phone. Those were always a great read, though he hated the redemptive endings. If only this very talented writer had the guts to follow his plots all the way, he himself might find an ecstasy he never knew.

Maybe he could contact him in about ten years and have him do a biography of Lawrence Whitney, hired killer, lover of dead women, friend to mankind. Deliver the message. *Here is your release, people. Everything you have done to restrain your deep inner natures has only made you miserable and sheepish. By this time you should know there is no ultimate good, as it is defined by the clerics and the fakers. The only good is what you yourself define now and live by. You've got to have the courage.*

What do you make of that, Mr. Coben?

And so he began sipping his drink, relaxing his muscles and his mind. When he did that, his subconscious would take over and formulate the plans going forward.

He let out a deep sigh and began to read.

CHAPTER TWENTY-SEVEN

"YNEZ?"

No answer.

"Ynez!" Keely's eyes were fixated on the man and the blood.

From a thousand miles away: "I'm on the phone."

"Come here now!"

Keely heard Ynez mumble some words and then her steps coming toward the room.

"What is it?" Ynez said. She came in. "I just have to finish this—"

The sound of her gasp was like a door creaking and slamming shut.

Ynez dropped her phone. She grabbed hold of Keely's arm. "What... what..."

"I just opened the closet," Keely said, her voice a whisper even though she hadn't intended it to be.

"Oh my—" Ynez bent forward, looking intently. She let go of Keely and took a couple of steps closer to the body.

Then she put her hand over her mouth and ran into the bathroom. Keely heard the awful sound of retching and almost lost her own cookies right there.

She went into the bathroom to help Ynez, who was on her

knees over the bowl. She finished her expulsions with an awful, final shriek.

There was a roll of paper towels on the sink. Keely ripped one and ran it under some water, squeezed out the excess. She got on her knees next to Ynez.

"Here, honey," Keely said. She applied the wet towel to Ynez's forehead.

"It ..."

"Don't talk yet."

Ynez grabbed Keely's wrist. "It's Buddy!"

THE NORTH LAS VEGAS homicide detective was named Rodney Blande. He was in his forties and shaped like a pear. He looked like no suit and tie would ever rest comfortably on his body, as exhibited by the gold-with-red-stripes tie askew on his torso.

"I need to ask you a few questions," Blande said. "I know this is difficult."

"Difficult!" Ynez said "How am I going to sell this house now? I have to disclose there was a dead body in the freaking closet!"

"You seem more upset about that than the fact that a man you know is dead."

"Look, Sherlock, he was a stalker. I had to get a restraining order to—"

She stopped herself. Keely knew why. If ever there was a motive for murder, a stalker with an RO was it.

"Are you questioning her as a suspect?" Keely said.

Detective shot her a look. "Excuse me. You don't have any standing here."

"Well I'm standing. Right here."

"That's not what I meant. You're interfering with an investigation."

"Tell me, Detective Blond—"

"Blande."

"How making sure my friend's rights under the Constitution are upheld, is interfering with an investigation?"

Man, that felt good.

"I can place you both under arrest now, and take you to the station for questioning. How would you like that?"

"And then you'll have to explain to your superior why you hauled in two innocent people just because you got a little hacked off at the Constitution."

The Constitution bit was very good. Maybe she should go to law school.

"You're not from around here, are you?" Detective Rodney Blande said.

"What does that have to do with anything?" Keely said.

"Maybe you don't know how we do things out here in the desert," Blande said.

"The Constitution doesn't apply to the desert?"

"It means we interpret it right," Blande said. "Not like big city lawyers."

Ynez said, "Keely, it's all right. I'm sure the detective here just wants to do his job and eliminate me as a suspect."

"Both of you," Blande said.

"Is this going to take long?" Keely said.

"I don't know," Blande said. "Up to you."

Keely tried not to roll her eyes, but they just couldn't help themselves.

"Look," Ynez said, "His name is Buddy Ricks and I dated him a few times. He wanted to get hot and heavy and I wanted to get cold and out of it. He wouldn't take no for an answer. So I did the right thing and I went to court and I got a restraining order, and that was the last of it until ..."

"Yes?" Blande said.

"About a week ago," Ynez said.

"What happened about a week ago?"

"I went to pick up my daughter from soccer practice, and saw him standing under a tree, watching her. He was supposed to stay three hundred yards away from me or Lucy. I was livid. I started for him but he ran away. Really, just ran like a scared puppy. And that was the last I saw of him until ... today."

Ynez placed her right hand over her eyes and rubbed.

"And what about you, Ms ... what was it?"

"Delmonico."

"You are here because?"

"I'm her friend."

"Your occupation?"

"Unemployed."

"Previous occupation?"

"Bagman for the mob," Keely said.

"You want to make this difficult, do you?"

"I don't see why we have to answer any more questions," Keely said. "You know everything."

"Do either of you own a gun?" Blande said.

"Come on!" Keely said.

"You want to answer the question?"

"No, I don't. But seeing as this is the Wild West, no, I don't own a gun."

"I do," Ynez said.

It didn't surprise Keely, but she wished it weren't so anyway. It meant another five minutes with this Blande.

Blande said, "What kind of gun is it?"

"A Ruger," Ynez said.

"Caliber?"

"Twenty-two."

"Where do you keep it?"

"At home. In a safe."

"Is it there now?"

"Of course it's there now! Are you kidding me with these questions?"

"I don't kid about murder," Blande said.

"When do you ever kid?" Keely said. "You must be a barrel of laughs at home."

A barb too far. Keely knew she'd overstepped even before Blande's cheeks pinkened.

"Turn around," he said.

"What?" Keely said.

"Turn around! Hands behind your back."

"No way!"

"You want a resisting charge added?"

Ynez stood. "This isn't necessary. We've told you everything."

"Stand aside," Blande said to Ynez.

Moving faster than Keely thought he could, Blande grabbed her left arm and twisted it behind her. A pain firecracker snapped in her shoulder. She felt the cuff on wrist and heard it snap-grind.

Blande grabbed her right arm and brought it back, cuffed that, too.

"Freaking ridiculous!" Keely said.

"Please, detective," Ynez said.

"You going to come along nicely?" Blande said.

"Where?" Ynez said.

"We're going to sort all this at the station."

"Are you arresting us?"

"This one I am," Blande said. "You want to join her?"

"This is unbelievable!" Ynez said.

"Believe it," Blande said.

The other detective stuck his head in the room. "Rod," he said, "can I see you a second?"

"Not now," Blande said.

"I think you better."

Blande paused, then said, "You two stay right here."

"I'm going to escape through the toilet," Keely said.

"I'll be watching," Blande said. He pulled out his gun and twirled it—actually twirled it, gunslinger style. Then he went outside the room, but turned back to it as his partner spoke softly in his ear.

"I just can't believe this," Ynez said. "I mean, he was a loser, but he didn't have to end up like that."

"Any idea who would want to kill him?"

Ynez thought about it. "He liked living on the edge."

"How do you know?"

"Because on our first date he said to me, 'I like living on the edge.'"

"Ah. But Ynez ..."

"What?"

"This isn't a coincidence, Buddy being here."

"What do you mean?"

Keely wasn't sure, but her mind was clicking along and she just followed. "I mean this was either meant to send you a message—"

"Don't say that," Ynez said.

"Well—"

"What was the other thing?"

Before Keely could answer, Detective Blande came back in the room. He was holding something.

"Look what we have here," Blande said. He held up a plastic evidence bag.

With a gun inside.

"It's a Ruger .22," Blande said. "What do you think of that?"

"That was the other thing," Keely said.

Ynez was speechless, staring.

"What are you talking about?" Blande said.

"Somebody is setting her up," Keely said.

"Oh really?"

"That can't be my gun," Ynez said. "Mine is still at my house, locked up."

"Why don't we go see?" Blande said.

CHAPTER TWENTY-EIGHT

WHAT WAS THAT all about?

Larry Whitney, relaxed now, had decided to take one more drive past the house. He'd stopped at the corner, though, when he saw the police cruiser parked outside.

The timing was perfect. A suit with detective written all over him got out, went around to the side, opened the door. A woman got out, some sort of professional. Latina, it looked like.

There was another head in the cruiser.

Keely Delmonico.

What was up indeed?

Larry Whitney could handle cops, as a lawyer. But as someone out for ecstasy, this cop development was troubling. Not fatal, but he'd have to run a few more scenarios in his mind before choosing the right course.

IT WAS THE STRANGEST FEELING. Like someone was watching her.

Well, Keely thought, she was cuffed in a police car. Some kids could be looking at her like she was a vicious criminal, a bank robber maybe.

But she saw no kids. And she could not turn around. Her seat belt was locked.

So welcome to Las Vegas, girl! Aren't you glad you came?

Blande's partner, whose name Keely had not picked up, was in the front seat looking at his phone. He was a bean compared to Blande's potato-like build.

"So you found the gun, huh?" Keely said.

The detective kept looking at his phone.

"You mind telling me where you found it?"

"Sorry, ma'am."

"Well at least you called me *ma'am*. A little respect going on. I like it."

The detective nodded, but at his phone.

"She didn't do this, you know."

"Ma'am?"

"She did not shoot that man. I've been with her all ..." She stopped, because that sounded like a lame excuse from a loyal friend. Of course Ynez could have done it, if she was stupid. Kill her stalker and then hide him in a closet in a house she was selling. Even these dunderheaded cops would figure that.

And yet, Ynez's gun was right there inside her house, in a safe.

So why was Ynez being led out of the house in handcuffs?

WHY WAS the dark chick being led out of the house in handcuffs?

Larry Whitney cursed, quietly, not desperately. This was an annoyance, nothing more. The cops were somehow involved with the two women, and that would make things a little more challenging.

Not that he ran from a challenge. It made the chase all the more exciting.

But he was not here on a solo mission, he had a phone to retake, and now it was looking like it might wind up in police custody.

That is, if Keely had it with her. There was always the chance she was keeping it hidden somewhere.

Or ...

She had to know by now it was locked and protected. She'd need either law enforcement or some private specialist to try to get at the information.

But now she was in Vegas, not L.A., and staying with this former call girl who was selling real estate.

Larry Whitney checked his notes, which he kept on a secure doc in his own phone. Ynez Ibarra worked for an outfit called Connor-Reilly Realty. These offices usually had some tech person working with their computers. Or else had a contract with a consultant.

He opened his to-do list. Larry Whitney loved to-do lists, kept them religiously. It's what made him great, he knew that. You prioritize your tasks each day. There are *High, Low,* and *Can Wait* tasks. The trick in life was to do the Highs first, and in order of importance, then move on to the Lows. Don't do any Can Waits if there's not time. Kick them down the road.

Right now, on his to-do list Larry put *Find computer guy at Connor-Reilly.*

He marked it *High.*

CHAPTER TWENTY-NINE

AT THE STATION THEY separated Keely from Ynez, sitting Keely in a too-cold room with just a couple of chairs and a table. Oh yes, and a camera hidden inside a mirrored glass ball.

Subtle.

Blande came in with a clipboard and an attitude. He tossed the clipboard on the desk. It made a clatter that echoed in the room.

He pulled out a chair and parked. "Your cooperation is appreciated," he said.

"I haven't cooperated yet," Keely said.

"You're here. I'm thanking you in advance."

"You can save it," Keely said. "You got this whole thing wrong and even you must know it."

"I only know what the facts give me. I want to go over those facts with you."

"Am I under arrest?"

"No."

"Then I want to leave."

"You're not free to leave. You are in temporary custody until I get some answers."

"Then you can advise me of my rights and I'll ask for a lawyer and I'll refuse to talk."

"Do you want to help your friend? The best way you can is by cooperating with me so we can clear this matter up. You are a witness. You found the body, is that right?"

Keely paused, considered what to do. The first time she'd been popped as a hooker a public defender told her the first and last rule was you never talked to a cop. Never, ever, unless he's a paying customer.

But she felt a desperation to get out of there so she could help Ynez. Nothing she could say would incriminate either one of them.

Still, it was difficult for her to say, "Yes, I found the body. You already know that."

"How long have you been in Las Vegas, Ms. Delmonico?"

"Since yesterday."

"Before that where were you?"

"I was in Los Angeles. That's where I live."

"Is there anyone who can vouch for your whereabouts in Los Angeles?"

"Sure."

"How did you get here?"

"Drove."

"And the reason for your visit?"

"To see my friend, who you are stupidly holding on a charge of murder."

Blande rubbed his forehead. "I don't appreciate that word."

"Murder?"

"Stupidly. You saw what happened. Your friend's gun was recovered on the property where the murder took place. Naturally we are going to go through ballistics, but doesn't it seem a little strange to you that a man she had a restraining order against ends up dead in a house that she is the listing agent for? And her gun is on the premises?"

"Her gun was in a safe, at her place."

Blande shook his head.

Keely said, "Where on the premises did you find it?"

"I'm not going to tell you that," Blande said.

"Oh, you are a sweet one," Keely said. "Listen, detective, how much sense does it make that someone would go to the trouble of killing a guy at a house she doesn't own and then hide the murder weapon there? And then leave the body in that same house even though the evidence points directly to her? And by the way, did you notice any blood stains on the carpet in the bedroom?"

"There weren't any bloodstains."

"Exactly. You would need to believe that Ynez somehow got Buddy to walk into a closet and quietly submit to getting shot."

A smile appeared on Blande's face. "Of course I know all this. You are pretty smart to notice those things."

"Well, I–"

"Which also makes you smart enough to help plan a murder that is set up to look so strange that it couldn't possibly be the person who actually committed the crime."

Keely slapped her hand on the desk. "Are you going to let me go or not? This is all I have to say on the matter. I came out from LA. to stay with Ynez, she was showing me around today, took me to this house she was selling to show me how she does things, and I found this guy's body in the closet. Unless Ynez is the greatest fake vomiter of all time, she had nothing to do with this. And neither did I. She has a daughter and I want to make sure the daughter's taken care of. Are you going to hold Ynez?"

"I'm afraid so, for now."

"I want to see her. I want to make sure she has a lawyer."

"You can see her in my presence."

"What a pleasure."

BLANDE BROUGHT Ynez to the interview room. He brought his chair around the desk for Ynez to sit in.

Ynez grasped Keely's hand. "I'm so sorry. You didn't need this."

"Do you know a lawyer?" Keely said.

"There's a lawyer in my networking group, Ken Blankenship."
Ynez looked at Blande. "Do I get a phone call?"

"Yes," said Blande.

"Lucy," Ynez said.

"I'll take care of her," Keely said.

"She's with her friend Alma. Pat, Alma's mother, might be able to take care of her for awhile."

"I'll see to it."

"What's going to happen next?" Ynez asked Blande.

"You'll be booked and taken to the NLV Detention Center."

"She's innocent!" Keely said.

"That's for the D.A. to decide."

Ynez squeezed Keely's hand. "Don't worry. God's got this. You and Lucy pray for me."

"Me?"

"It's easy," Ynez said. "Lucy will show you how."

KEELY INSISTED SOMEBODY drive her back to Ynez's house. Blande said she could not insist on that. Keely said she just did, and did he want her to make a federal case out of it?

He told her to sit and wait on a bench by the front desk and he'd see what he could do.

Keely put in a call to Amy Matsumoto.

"Hey," Amy said, "where are you?"

"Vegas."

"Oh man," Amy said. "I'm so sorry."

"Sorry about what?"

"You haven't heard?"

"Heard *what?*"

"Oh no."

Keely said, "Talk to me."

"The woman you work for, Madam V?"

"What about Madam V?"

"She's dead."

For a moment, Keely couldn't move.

"I'm so sorry," Amy said. "I know you liked her."

"How?" Keely said.

"They didn't say. Just that she was found. It's all over local news."

"They arrest anybody?"

"Uh-uh. No suspect yet."

But Keely had a suspect. It was him. He'd gotten to Madam V. She wouldn't have told him.

Would she?

There are ways to make anybody talk.

"Keely?"

"Yeah?"

"You gonna be okay?"

"Goodbye, Amy."

CHAPTER THIRTY

KEELY PULLED INTO THE driveway of a house that looked like pretty much every other house on the block.

A woman answered her knock. She had red hair and green eyes, was a little on the plump side, had an easy smile. "Keely?"

"That's me," Keely said.

"I'm Pat. Come on in."

The house had surroundings. The sound of a TV came from another room and two girl voices talked over it.

Pat said, "Lucy and Alma are watching a movie." She laughed and added, "Or not."

"I have something I need to tell you," Keely said.

"Is something wrong?"

"Oh yeah. Where can we talk without the girls hearing?"

Pat said, "Really?"

Keely said, "Really."

Pat led her into the kitchen.

Keely said, "Ynez is in jail."

"Oh, no," Pat said. "I knew it was going to happen."

"You knew?"

"She never pays her tickets. I kept telling her they weren't going to just let them go. Did they take her license?"

"It's not that," Keely said. "It's a whole lot worse."

"Worse?"

"Did you know Buddy Ricks?" Keely said.

"Scumbag."

"Ynez and I found his body in a house she's selling."

Pat did not say anything.

"The police are holding her as a suspect," Keely said.

"No way. She wouldn't do that, or maybe she would if he was trying to attack her. Is that what happened?"

Keely shook her head. "She was shocked to see him there."

"What was he doing in that house she was selling?"

"We don't know the answer to that. But we're taking steps. She knows a lawyer–"

"Right, Ken Blankenship."

"Is he good?" Keely said.

"I think so. He has a good reputation."

"So until we can get this straightened out, can Lucy stay here with you?"

"Of course. But what are we going to tell her?"

"Let me take a stab at it," Keely said, then added, "Wrong choice of words."

Pat put her hand on Keely's. "You want to tell her now?"

Keely knocked back the rest of her drink. The bourbon burned on the way down. "Why not?"

KEELY TOOK Lucy to the back yard, where they sat on a lounge swing. The chain squeaked as Keely pushed, gently. Lucy's feet did not reach the ground.

"How would you like to spend the night with Alma?" Keely asked.

"I have to ask my mom," Lucy said.

"I've talked to your mom. It's okay."

"Really?'

"Yep."

"Cool. Are you and my mom going somewhere?"

"Not tonight," Keely said. "Listen, you know how sometimes people make mistakes, big old mistakes?"

Lucy nodded uncertainly.

"You know, like Amanda Bynes on Twitter?"

"Who?"

"Look, even people who aren't supposed to make mistakes do it sometimes, like police."

"Oh."

"Well, they made a mistake today, the police did. See, they think your mom did something, and they want to talk to her about it."

Lucy spun to face Keely. "The police?"

"Yeah."

"Why?"

"Well, they have a job to do, and they just need to clear things up."

"Where's my mom?"

"She's down at the police station."

"Is she coming home?"

"Well, not right away."

"Why?"

"Something happened in one of the houses she's selling," Keely said. "You know how that is?"

Lucy nodded. "One time the carpet was all dirty and she had to call somebody to clean it up."

"Yes," Keely said. "Something like that. Your mom told me to tell you to pray, so it all gets cleared up."

"Okay." Lucy leaned over and kissed Keely on the cheek.

"What was that for?" Keely said.

"Because I like you," Lucy said.

CHAPTER THIRTY-ONE

THERE WERE ONLY TWO men who had Larry Whitney's new phone number. One of them was his older brother, Casey, who would only use it when he was in trouble. Casey was a junkie and petty criminal who had once been the smart one in the family. Even had a job in New York at Morgan Stanley for awhile. Then he started on the booze and his wife left him and took the two kids, and then he got sacked and went to heroin and that was that.

Larry Whitney was his last link with anything resembling reality. Larry was of the school that said if you turn your life into road kill don't ask me to clean it up. But Larry sent him money sometimes when Casey called, even though he knew the money would go right to a needle and into Casey's arm.

It also struck him that the only true aliveness Casey felt was when he was amped, the way Larry felt when he took forbidden flesh after a fresh kill.

Yeah, a brother like that could have his phone number, even with a burner.

The other person who had his phone number was the front man on this contract, and that was who was calling him now.

"That you?" Tim McGinnis said. He did not know Larry's name, which is how Larry always played it.

"It is," Larry said. He was parked in his car in the lot outside the office building wherein worked one Jude Andreu.

"I haven't heard from you," Tim McGinnis said.

"That's because I haven't called."

"Where are you?"

"Out of town."

"What?"

"I'm after the asset."

"What happened? You were supposed–"

"I am going to bring home the asset. Leave it to me."

"What went wrong?"

"You're assuming something went wrong," Larry said.

"That's right," Tim McGinnis said. He sounded like a desperate man. Always bad for business.

"I will wrap this up," Larry said. "So don't call me again."

"Why not?"

"I'll call you."

"Listen, I–"

Larry killed the call.

Good timing, too, because Jude the computer guy was coming out the side door. He had a backpack over one shoulder, graduate-student style, and was fumbling with his car keys.

CHAPTER THIRTY-TWO

BACK AT YNEZ'S KEELY looked up the office of Kenneth Blankenship, Attorney-at-Law. She used Ynez's landline to call the number and got his voicemail.

"This is Ynez Ibarra's friend, Keely. I'm at Ynez's house. I just wanted to follow-up to make sure Ynez got hold of you. She's in jail at the North Las Vegas station. It's serious. Please call back so I know you two have connected."

Alone in Ynez's house, she felt like an intruder in someone's normal world. The weird character in a sitcom who comes in for an episode and throws everything into turmoil.

She went into the kitchen and opened the fridge. There was half a bottle of white zin in the door. She helped herself to a glass. Then spotted a pad and pen on the counter. The pad was one of those long skinny things with a realtor's picture and logo on it. Ynez smiled at her from the pad. Her head was slightly cocked, her smile wide. *Call Ynez Ibarra and Start Packing!*

Keely sat on the sofa in the living room, turned on the TV and found a Sirius station pumping classic pop. Her grandmother's era. Jo Stafford was singing "You Belong To Me."

She put her wine glass on a coaster on the coffee table, picked up the pad and pen.

Puzzle it out, she told herself, and started to make notes.

Body in the closet.

Shot in the back of the head.

No blood on the carpet.

Obvious set-up (house Ynez is selling)

Why?

Buddy into something.

Meant to scare Ynez.

Motive. Money, sex, power.

She put a line through *sex* and *power*.

Follow the money.

As she picked up her wine glass she almost dropped it when Ynez's phone clamored.

"Ken Blankenship," the voice said. "Returning your call."

"Ah. Good. Thank you."

"I was just with Ynez. She's going to be spending the weekend in jail."

"But why?"

"Arrested on a Friday. There won't be a bail hearing till Monday."

"That stinks!"

"Yeah, it does. Sometimes cops plan it that way." His voice was deep and confident with a bit of street in it.

"She didn't do it," Keely said.

"I know," Blankenship said.

"How do you know?"

"I know Ynez. And now I want to know you. You're a key witness."

"That's right." Keely took a healthy sip of wine.

"Can you walk me through what happened?" Blankenship said.

She did, from the moment Ynez took her to the real estate office, to the finding of the body.

When Keely was finished Blankenship said, "Tell me a little about yourself, Keely. You're from L.A., you were friends with Ynez?"

"Sort of."

"What's that mean?"

"I knew her. I liked her. We weren't real close."

"You knew her through Madam V."

Pause. Then: "Ynez told you about all that?"

"She didn't have to," Blankenship said. "I know about her back-ground. I'm her lawyer. And just so you know, it means nothing to me. But if you are deposed, or have to testify, it's likely to come out."

"Great! I hope the trial will be on TV, too."

"That's not going to happen," Blankenship said.

"This is a freaking nightmare." She rubbed the bridge of her nose to hold off pain racing to her forehead. "Are you my lawyer, too?"

"You're not charged with anything."

"I mean, can I tell you something and it will be, uh, confidential?"

"Technically, I can't say our conversation is protected. I'm taking notes. But if you want to tell me something I will conveniently forget to take notes, and what you say will be just between us."

Keely took a deep breath and a long sip of wine. "Okay, I have a reason I don't want to make any noise. There are people who would like to find me and I don't want to be found."

After a pause, Blankenship said, "I understand, believe me. I've had a client or two who's been in that situation. This is Las Vegas, after all. So if it comes down to it, I can assist you in that."

A small but warm relief blew through Keely. Having someone on her side, who could actually help, felt good. She also knew that she'd grab for any life preserver floating by, even a lawyer she'd just now gotten to know.

"First thing," Keely said, "is getting Ynez out of this."

"Right," Blankenship said. "And you're going to be an integral part of it. You said you're at Ynez's."

"Yeah."

"Lucy is at her friend's?"

"Yes."

"All right, can you meet with my team tomorrow?"

"You have a team?"

He laughed. "Every high-flying, unbeatable lawyer has a team."

Keely smiled. Somehow he had managed to ease her nerves for a moment. "Yes," she said. "Where and what time?"

"Let me set things up. I'll call you in the morning. How are you fixed for money?"

"I'm not rolling in it, but I'm fine."

"Put it all on red."

"What?

"Kidding. We're not gambling here, not with Ynez, and not with you. I'll be in touch."

CHAPTER THIRTY-THREE

NORMALCY.

Shower. Good coffee. Toast.

No cigarette, though. Keely chewed on a plastic straw instead.

At nine she drove to the police station to see Ynez. After passing through the detectors and getting wanded for good measure, Keely was given fifteen minutes in the holding cell. Ynez was still in yesterday's clothes and looked like she'd just awakened on a park bench.

"I talked to Blankenship," Keely said. "I'm going to meet with him later."

"Good. He told me no bail till Monday."

"They're treating you like Bonnie."

"Like who?"

"You know, Bonnie and Clyde."

Ynez sighed. "Did you talk to Lucy?"

"I did," Keely said.

"How'd she take it?"

"She wants to see you."

"Let's see about bail first. I'd rather see her at home."

"Can I bring you anything?"

Ynez said, "Some clothes, underwear. They said I could have a bag. Toothbrush. Makeup. I must look like flaming death."

"No, no," Keely said. "Not flaming."

"And my Bible. It's on my night stand."

"Got it."

"Why would somebody do this?" Ynez said.

"We'll figure it out. It's got to be somebody trying to get at you, through Buddy. What was he into?"

Shaking her head, Ynez said, "I'm not really sure. He liked to spend money, show it off, but I never knew exactly what he did. I don't think he did any one thing."

"Gambler?"

"Probably. He liked to dress like a cowboy, only not a real cowboy, with dirt on his jeans, but some pretty boy playing cowboy."

"How'd you get involved?" Keely said.

"He was funny and charming," Ynez said. "He had this way about him. But it wore thin pretty quick. After he talked about himself which was, like, always, he had nothing more to say. When I told him to ride his horse somewhere else, he started with the insults and then following me around. I had to get a court order."

"But nothing about who his friends were, people he hung around with?"

Ynez shook her head.

"Anything you'd like me to tell the lawyer?" Keely said.

"Just tell him to win," Ynez said.

CHAPTER THIRTY-FOUR

KEELY WAS IN the lobby of the office building, looking at the directory, when she was tapped on the shoulder.

She turned around and was stunned.

Standing before her was the most drop-dead gorgeous woman she had ever seen.

No, that wasn't good enough. She was drop-dead-get-cremated-and-have-your-ashes-scattered-over-the-Alps gorgeous.

Tall, blonde, her hair like corn silk, which Keely had seen on her grandmother's farm and even tried to smoke once. The woman's figure may have been sculpted by the finest and most design-worthy surgeon in the world, though Keely thought it was natural, because her face was so flawless. She was wearing a white dress that held her body like a mother caressing a child.

"You are Ms. Delmonico?" she asked in a voice with a slight Eastern European accent, the kind that would push men over the edge who had already gone crazy looking at her stunningness.

Keely nodded.

"You are here for Mr. Blankenship?"

"That's right."

"If you wouldn't mind coming with me?"

Keely followed her through the ornate lobby. Heads turned like Swiss clockworks. How could they not? Keely imagined this woman had to go through this wherever she went. She'd probably knock out the security system at any 7-Eleven as well as get a ball-room of diplomats to stop chattering and just stare.

They passed a bank of elevators and went around the corner to a single elevator with a copper-colored door. The woman held a card up to a smooth rectangular panel attached to the wall. The elevator doors opened. The woman put her arm out and Keely stepped into the elevator. The woman followed and held the card against a panel of three buttons. The elevator started to go up.

"How do you like Las Vegas?" the woman said.

"It's changed a bit since I was here last," Keely said.

"We've heard that."

"I don't mean to pry," Keely said. "But what exactly do you do for Mr. Blankenship?"

"I don't actually work for Mr. Blankenship. I work for someone else. Personal assistant."

"You should be in movies, if you don't mind my saying."

"That life does not interest me."

Keely said, "Well, that's kind of refreshing."

"Here we are."

The elevator opened up into a reception area that could have been the first floor of one of those palaces from the old French king days. Everything was marble and gold inlay and modern artwork and windows. A man sitting at the reception desk looked ex-military. He nodded at Beautiful and just looked at Keely. Though he did smile. Keely smiled back but it felt like her mouth was fighting her. What her mouth really wanted to do was shout *Holy crap!*

The man behind the desk hit a buzzer and Beautiful pushed open a door the size of a garage. Inside was an office not so large as the reception area, but every bit as impressive. There was a huge window behind the desk and an executive chair with its back to

Keely. Whoever was in the chair was looking out the window at the skyline of Las Vegas while talking to someone on the phone.

"That will be fine," he said. "I'll plan on flying out on Wednesday, and we'll stay at The Lodge. You like that? We'll play eighteen on Thursday. Supposed to be perfect weather. Then we'll have the next two days to ourselves. How's that sound?"

Beautiful looked at Keely and smiled, as if to say this is what I go through all the time. I wait for the man—whoever this man was—to finish what he's doing. Only then do I get an audience.

"Right," the man said. "You too, babe. Bye."

The executive chair turned around.

The man was around fifty. He wore a crisp white shirt and perfectly knotted gold tie. Keely wondered if it might have actual gold in it.

His hair was tight steel curls and he had a tan that was clearly from a booth. Meaning deep and even. He put his phone on the desk next to a framed photo of two girls and a woman. A family man.

He stood and extended his hand. "Ms. Delmonico?"

Keely said, "Yes" and shook his hand.

"Gary Stoddard," he said. "Please have a seat."

There was a chair to her right. Keely sat in it.

"You've met Brigita," he said.

Perfect, Keely thought. That's exactly the name she should have.

"Yes," said Keely.

"Can she get you anything to drink?" Stoddard said.

"I think I'm good," Keely said.

"Well, you just let me know if you change your mind. Thank you, Brigita."

Brigita nodded and left the office.

"Wow," Keely said.

"Indeed," Stoddard said. "She has a Masters degree in criminal justice."

"Not just another pretty face, huh?"

Stoddard folded his hands on the desk. "Now, I understand your good friend is in jail, accused of murder?"

Keely swallowed. "That's right. Is Mr. Blankenship here?"

"I'm handling this part of it."

"There's parts?"

"Oh, yes," Stoddard said. "Now, your friend has a daughter?"

"Lucy."

"And you would like to see her out as quickly as possible," Stoddard said.

"Of course," Keely said. "She didn't do it."

"I know."

It was very cool the way he said it, just like a high-powered lawyer should. She was starting to relax.

"The thing is," Stoddard said, "like everything else in Vegas, it all comes down to money." He smiled. "But that's not such a bad thing. It makes it easy to keep score."

"My understanding is that Mr. Blankenship is a friend of Ynez's. I sort of got the feeling he was going to handle this for free."

"You mean the criminal matter?" Stoddard said. "Yes, I think that's the arrangement. But as far as the money, we were hoping you could help."

Keely looked at the blue eyes of Gary Stoddard, which seemed to have switched the color of sky to a tint of ice.

"Can I ask what money you're referring to?" Keely said.

"Nine hundred thousand," Stoddard said. "It's what Buddy Ricks owes us."

"He was your client?" Keely said.

"More of a debtor," Stoddard said. "The bad kind. The kind we call a deadbeat. He just refused to pay."

The afternoon sun was bouncing off the window of a large hotel a few blocks away, causing the light to change in Stoddard's office. A little darker now, like twilight.

"Wait a minute," Keely said. "Are you talking about legal fees?"

Stoddard shook his head.

Uh-oh.

"You ..." Keely said before her voice stopped working.

"Yes," Stoddard said. "I have settled with Mr. Ricks. And if you want to help your friend go free, you both will need to settle with us."

CHAPTER THIRTY-FIVE

FROM A VALLEY DEEP inside her, her voice barely an echo, Keely said, "Are you really saying you ...?"

"What, exactly?" Stoddard said.

"Killed Buddy Ricks?"

"I did not say that."

"I think you did."

"I said we *settled* with him."

"And I know exactly what that means."

"In any event, what you will understand from this point forward is much more important. Your friend is facing very serious charges. We know she has no alibi. We know where she was when the ... settlement took place."

"But I thought you said you didn't do it."

"You need to stop telling me what you think I said. Now, if you want your friend to go free, it can be arranged. For a fee."

Keely licked her bottom lip. It stayed dry. "It's going to cost a mil, right?"

"Nine hundred thousand, rounded down from the interest."

"Well, sure! Let me get my checkbook!"

Stoddard gave her a long, lingering look. "I want you to know that we are not unreasonable. We've also been known to be creative."

"Cement shoes?"

Shut up, Keely, just shut up!

"That was back in the old days," said Stoddard. "I remember my grandfather telling me about a real case of that kind of footwear. But that's really the realm of B movies and crime novels."

Stoddard got up and spun his chair around. It did a couple of revolutions and stopped. He went to the big window and put his hands behind him and looked out.

"What if we made it five hundred thousand on the financial side?"

He turned. "And then you come work for me?"

"Excuse me?"

"Work. For me."

Okay, Bizarro world. Keely couldn't think of a thing to say. She tried to keep her face from looking like she'd just been slapped with a flounder.

"I'm serious," Stoddard said. "I know you're qualified."

"How can you know anything about me?"

He sat on the corner of the desk, like a professor with an uncertain student. "As important as money is, information is just as valuable. Sometimes more. I make it my business to know about the people who come into my office. You were a professional gal, back in L.A. High end. Am I right?"

Was there no end to having her past wrap around her present?

"I run a business here that also has a high-end clientele. I'm talking from all over the world. Asia, the Middle East, Australia. You know Aussies are some of the nicest people in the world. You'd like them."

"You want me to be one of your rentals?"

"That's a very imprecise term. Not at all what I had in mind. You would be on salary. Full benefits—medical, dental—and not the crappy kind everyone else has to settle for. I'm talking top hospitals and doctors, even plastic surgeons if you're of a mind. And then there's the retirement package."

"You actually have a retirement package for hookers?"

"Again, not the term I would use. Professional Services Administrator. You'll have the finest clothes, the best food. You'll travel by private jet to Monaco, Cabo, all sorts of places. You will not find an opportunity like this anywhere else in your lifetime."

"So what's the catch?" Keely said. "Sign my name in blood? Sell my soul to the devil?"

"You don't believe in the devil, do you?"

"I'm thinking it over."

"I assure you, Ms. Delmonico, I am no devil. I am a businessman, a good one. One of the best. I could run for president of the United States, but I wouldn't want to descend to that level."

"Even if," Keely said, "what about the five hundred grand?"

"Ah, good for you. Back to basics." Stoddard stood up and returned to his chair. All business now. "That is your ticket to entry, and also the ticket for your friend to stay out of prison. That's exactly where she's going. I think you can see that."

"But how do you expect me to get hold of that kind of money?"

"That's where your own creativity comes in," Stoddard said. "I've learned over the years that if you give someone an impossible task, but also leave them with an inevitable—and highly undesirable—alternative, they almost always figure out a way. You figure it out, and everything will be taken care of."

Keely cleared her throat. It needed clearing, badly. "Am I just supposed to trust you on this?"

"Yes," Stoddard said. "It's the whole thing about leverage. You and your friend have none. You'll have to trust me. Even as I say I am a man of my word. I am, Ms. Delmonico. Truly. And just to show you I am, I'm going to spot you a couple of Cs. I know you need walking around money."

He opened a drawer and removed two bills. Hundreds. He placed them on the desk in front of Keely.

"And please remember, no going to the cops or the feds. You

must know I have anticipated all that, and am completely protected. If you try something foolish your friend is going to the jug, as they used to say. And her little girl will grow up being taunted by her little friends. I don't want to see that happen. I have a girl of my own, at Stanford. She is very well adjusted."

CHAPTER THIRTY-SIX

KEELY, NUMB AS AN ice sculpture, got into the elevator. It was one of those that had mirrors on both sides. Funny, she hadn't noticed it before, so taken she was with Brigita the Beautiful.

Now it was only her, and because of the reflections, her with a billion Keelys, on and on forever.

And which one of those was the real her?

She had no idea.

Every Keely was as distant and mysterious as an echo, as unknowable as the stars.

What if she let them absorb her? Where would she go? Would it mean no more pain in this world?

Escape.

But then, no. She wasn't about to go anywhere. She had Ynez and Lucy to care for. She had things left to do.

Hang on with both hands, Keely.

Hang on.

OUTSIDE, the sun was just about gone, but the dry heat lingered. It would last the night, go into the next morning, and then come back again after the day's fry was over.

Keely went to her car in the parking lot, unlocked it, got in and opened all the windows. She got out and leaned against the hood and looked at the traffic on the street.

She tried to make sense of what just went on.

Five hundred thousand dollars.

Seriously?

She had no doubt Stoddard was indeed serious. But what about Ken Blankenship? Some lawyer. Maybe he thought this was the best deal on the table.

Maybe, in fact, he was right.

Or maybe he was a scum.

She called him. And he answered.

"You scum," she said.

"What a way to talk," he said.

"You set this all up."

"I set up nothing. I'm a fixer. I'm fixing a very serious problem for Ynez."

A semi-truck thundered by on the road, grinding out noise. Keely held the phone over her left ear and closed off her other ear with her index finger. She shouted, "But she's not guilty!"

"We know that. But that doesn't matter to the people involved."

"Who you work for."

"No, Keely. I work *with* them. They help me, I help them, and in this case I'm helping everybody."

"You don't have an ego problem, do you?"

"All great lawyers have ego," Blankenship said. "You can't win without it. So what I'm telling you is think like the real world."

"So I'm supposed to raise five hundred thousand and rent myself out as a sex slave?"

"You would be a salaried employee. And let's face it, you are highly qualified."

"I want to punch you in the face."

"Maybe I could use it," he said. "But that won't help Ynez."

"How am I supposed to raise five hundred thousand dollars?"

"There could be a way," Blankenship said.

"What way?"

"I might be able to put together a deal."

"A *deal?* You're talking a deal?"

"It's what I do. If you're willing to roll the dice, I'm—"

"Oh shut up! Don't give me any stupid Las Vegas talk. I'm telling you, if you do anything that hurts Ynez, I will hurt you."

"I understand how you feel," Blankenship said.

"No you don't," Keely said.

"Why don't we have a nice drink and discuss the deets."

"Did you just say *deets?*"

"Uh-huh."

"Well don't! I don't want to talk to a school kid."

"I like you," Blankenship said.

A mix of loathing and respect filled her, not the kind of respect that you honor but that you acknowledge because it can get things done.

But did she want that kind of help?

What choice did she have? To help Ynez, and Lucy.

There was no way out.

She said, "Oh goodie, you just made my day. I can't wait to discuss the deets."

CHAPTER THIRTY-SEVEN

AND BEFORE HER DAY would be complete, sure, yeah, a drink with Blankenship, she rolled to Connor-Reilly to see if she could scare up the computer whiz.

There was no one at the front desk.

A man in a cubicle was talking and gesturing in front of a computer monitor.

Keely was about to stroll back to the computer room when Ezra Hirsch, the managing partner she'd met with Ynez, came out of his office. He was dressed Saturday casual, shorts and a polo shirt. He was holding a folder that had a nighttime picture of Las Vegas on the front.

"Oh, hey," he said, not entirely friendly. Then he perked. "I left a message for Ynez. She hasn't called back."

"Uh, yeah," Keely said. "She's a bit tied up at the moment."

"One of her clients is trying to get hold of her."

"Ah."

"So where is she?"

Keely sighed. He was going to find out anyway. "A man who was stalking her wound up dead. So the cops want to question Ynez about it."

"What?"

"I've been with her. She didn't do it, but they don't know who did."

"So where is she?"

"Jail."

"Jail!"

"For the weekend," Keely said.

Hirsch slapped his sides. "That makes it a little difficult for her to conduct her business."

"Hey man, she's in jail. For doing nothing. Help her out."

"I'm just saying—"

"Well don't just say.'

"Listen Ms...I forgot your name."

"Fury."

"What?"

"Fury Rage, that's my name."

Ezra Hirsch pursed his lips.

"So now you know," Keely said. "Help her out. Run a little interference for her."

"I'll do what I can," he said.

"Thank you. Is Jude in?"

"No, as a matter of fact."

"You expecting him?"

"He comes in early on Saturday, stays till about noon. He didn't come in today."

"Can we call him?"

"Why?"

"He was doing something for me, on the side."

"Look, Ms. ..., this is a place of business. I can't be chasing people down."

"Well just give me his phone number."

"I can't do that."

"What do you mean?"

"I mean, we don't do that around here. Jail? Really?"

"I kind of need to talk to him."

He looked at his watch. Sighed. "Why don't you give me your number? If I hear from him, I'll have him give you call."

"Well thanks whole bunches."

"You don't have to be rude about it," he said.

"I know I don't have to," she said, "but the desire is just springing up inside me."

SHE WAS to meet Blankenship in a lounge bar near Planet Hollywood. The place was packed with up-scale professionals, buffed-out gym rats and tightly-dressed cleavage hussies. Dance-pop pumped through the pink and peaches interior with its three levels. The ground floor was dazzle. The second looked like glitter. Keely didn't care what was on any third level.

What she wanted was to find Blankenship, hear his pitch, and get out of there.

An Asian hostess made a beeline for her. "Are you here to see Mr. Blankenship?"

"Is there anybody in this town who doesn't know who I'm seeing?"

The hostess smiled, but there was nothing going on behind the eyes.

"Yes," Keely said. "Blankenship."

"Ah," she said with apparent relief, "this way."

Ken Blankenship looked like a frat boy. He was probably late thirties but had the shaggy sandy hair of a member of Tappa Kegga Brew about to watch football. He had on a gray sport coat and black slacks, a maroon tie loosened under an unbuttoned collar. But the worst of all was his eager, I'm-cool-how-about-you smile.

He got up from the horseshoe booth. "Keely?"

She shook his hand. It was soft.

He sat with a sigh, like he'd been out plowing farmland. "What are you drinking?"

"Hemlock."

Smiling, he said, "How about a Volcanic Ash? It's their signature—"

"I'm not here to enjoy myself," Keely said.

"Come on," Blankenship said. "What is this life if you can't have a little fun and do business at the same time?"

"I don't like your kind of business."

"Honey," he said, putting his elbows on the table, "there's only business that wins and business that loses. Take your pick."

A waitress in a come-hither pink dress asked what they'd like to drink. Blankenship deferred to Keely. She said, "Coke."

"That's it?" Blankenship said.

"With a slice of lemon," Keely said.

"Bring me a double Jack, neat," Blankenship said.

The waitress catwalked away.

"So," Keely said, "business."

"Right." Blankenship laced his fingers together on the table. "The issue is the five hundred thousand—"

"No, the issue is removing the frame from Ynez Ibarra."

"That's the relief you seek. To get that relief, you need to get your hands on the money."

"Whatever."

"Exactly. Whatever it takes, right? But here's the nice thing. You already know how to do it."

He smiled without teeth—the self-satisfied way.

Which once again made Keely want to hit him in the face.

Which would not help Ynez.

She just stared at him until the smile faded.

"Here it is," Blankenship said. "A certain hotel has an interest in pleasing its favorite whales. One of them in particular. Some kind of royalty. Likes to have some candy on his arm, and then in his bed. He's very particular about that part of the arrangement."

"Uh-huh."

"Do you see where I'm going?" Blankenship said.

"Like you had headlights," Keely said. "But where's the five hundred come in?"

"Let's suppose that this particular roller drops a certain number before going home. If he could be convinced to stay and keep on rolling, that would be of interest to this certain hotel casino."

"So I'm the convincer?"

"I think you're just the one."

"And how does that help me?"

"A percentage of what he drops will be credited to your account."

"Unbelievable."

"Plus, this whale has been known to shower gifts on the women that please him. I'm talking diamonds and every other kind of glittering doo-dad. You will pass those through to us and we will credit you the fair market value, less ten percent."

"This just keeps getting better."

The waitress came back with the drinks. Keely's Coke was flat and had no lemon slice.

Figured.

Ken Blankenship rammed half his bourbon.

Smiled.

"I don't get it," Keely said. "All this might take forever, and Ynez goes through hell."

"We are not unreasonable," Blankenship said. "We are willing to take a flyer on you, in good faith."

"It's kind of amazing to hear *good faith* coming out of your mouth."

"Keely, you've been around the block. Several blocks, I'm guessing. So what I find amazing is that you can be so naive."

He was right. This was the real world.

"Have I got your attention?" Blankenship said.

"Yes."

"You ready to rest your mouth?"

Keely gave her mouth some flat Coke.

"Okay," he said. "You start tonight."

"Tonight!"

"And Ynez walks on Monday."

Head throbbing like the beat of the music, Keely said, "But what if I don't ... what if he doesn't ..."

"Relax. You'll figure it out."

"I'm just saying."

"Only don't try to take advantage of the situation," he said. "I mean, we do have enforcement mechanisms."

Keely waited.

Blankenship finished his drink.

CHAPTER THIRTY-EIGHT

BRIGITA THE BEAUTIFUL GOT Keely in a killer dress from the shop in the hotel. Looking in the mirror, Keely felt like a frog next to a princess. But after the makeup from a woman Brigita called in, she decided no, it wasn't bad. Maybe she could come in a close second.

The Nordic assistant had not said much at all during the prep. All business. Nice, but quiet. Efficient. She could probably make all of Europe's trains run on time if given the power.

But then she took Keely into a small office at the back of the hotel. There was a simple pine desk with a bouquet of fresh flowers on it. And not much else. Brigita sat behind the desk, Keely in front.

"His name is Zainul Al-Kassanai. You will not address him personally until he gives you permission."

"Is this for real?"

"Absolutely."

"Where's this guy from?"

"Brunei," Brigita said.

"Where?" Keely said.

"It is part of the island of Borneo."

"Yeah? And where the freak is Borneo?"

"Malaysia."

"And where the—"

"South China Sea," Brigita said.

"And this guy comes all the way to Vegas to gamble?" Keely said.

"He is very taken with Penn and Teller," Brigita said. "And he likes the weather. But most of all, the action. His game is craps."

"I don't know the first thing about craps."

"You don't have to. You hang onto his arm and blow on the dice when he wants you to. You also jump up and down and yell a little when he wins."

"And when he loses?"

"Pout."

"Jeez."

"And if he is pleased with you, he will let you call him by his nickname."

"Please don't let it be Pinky."

"Pinky?"

"Never mind."

"It's Mitch," Brigita said.

"Mitch?"

"Actually, if he invites you, you will call him Mr. Mitch."

"You have got to be kidding," Keely said.

"He likes American movies. He especially loves Robert Mitchum."

Keely shook her head, feeling more and more like Alice halfway down the rabbit hole, and picking up speed.

A familiar voice came into her head, her own voice, cold and without feeling, the voice that would tell her it was her job, her body was her trade, she was good at her trade, and the money she made was earned. It was a voice used to drown out the loathing, and now it was back. Old friend.

Brigita said, "He has certain preferences in the bedroom, of course, but those will be made known to you in due course."

"I can hardly wait," Keely said.

"He is a lavish spender, as you know."

"Joy."

Brigita got up from behind the desk and came around and sat in the chair next to Keely. She put her hand on Keely's arm. "It's going to be all right," Brigita said. "I know this isn't an easy situation for you, but I will tell you that you can absolutely trust Mr. Stoddard. And me."

"Thanks. I think."

"All will be well," said Brigita, patting Keely's arm. "In half an hour, I will introduce you. Any questions?"

"Yeah," Keely said. "Do you like your life?"

The beautiful one sat back in her chair. For a long moment she didn't speak. Finally, she said, "I don't think it's a matter of liking. It's a matter of getting by. You do it any way you can."

"Cheery," Keely said.

CHAPTER THIRTY-NINE

HAJI ZAINUL AL-KASSANAI was five-and-a-half feet tall. His hair was black, his skin almond. Circling his mouth was a ring of neatly-trimmed hair, which in a fuller version might have resembled a goatee. His stomach was ample, pressing against the restraint of the vest of his gray, three-piece suit. He was nicely dressed for a short fat man, Keely thought.

Behind Al-Kassanai stood a large, unsmiling, in-shape, black-suited man with his hands folded in front of him, bodyguard-style. Keely briefly made eye contact with him. He looked like he wanted to chew on her ribs.

Brigita introduced Keely to Al-Kassanai. She put her hand out. Al-Kassanai's eyes widened. Brigita softly pushed Keely's arm down.

At this the fat whale smiled perfect white teeth, and held up two hands balled into fists.

On each of his fingers was a black letter. The fingers of the left hand had H-A-T-E on them. On the right was L-O-V-E

"You like?" Al-Kassanai said in a somewhat high, accented voice.

"Sure," Keely said.

"I have used only a pen," he said.

"Fine with me," Keely said.

"Do you know the story?"

"Story?"

"Good and evil," Al-Kassanai said, carefully forming the words. "It was with the left that Cain hit his brother down. The right hand has veins that go to the soul of man."

He laced his fingers together. "I will show you the story of life. Old brother left hand is fighting." He bent the left over the right. "It looks like love is a goner. But wait!" Now the right bent over the left. "Hot dog, love is winning. Yessirree. Hate is down for the ..."

He frowned.

"Down for the count?" Keely said.

"Yes!" Al-Kassanai said. "You know it!"

"I do?"

"It is what Robert Mitchum says in *Night of the Hunter.* Remember?"

"I don't think I've seen that one," Keely said.

"Oh, but you must! And you will! But not tonight. Tonight we play. Are you ready?"

"Hot dog," Keely said.

THE CASINO WAS HOPPING. Blackjack and crap tables, roulette and a Big Six wheel, slots and other blinking machines, all under chandeliers.

Al-Kassanai had offered his arm to Keely, and they were walking—well, she was walking, he was strutting—past all the gaming tables, toward the back of the casino. Mr. Bodyguard was behind them, a presence Keely could feel without turning around. Her job was to look good and get heads to turn.

Which they did.

At the end of a crap table a middle-aged man in a suit and fancy cowboy hat almost unscrewed his head as he gaped. He said,

"Oo-wee!" A middle-aged woman standing next to him glanced Keely's way then hit the man in the side with her right fist.

"Just window shoppin'!" the man said.

Al-Kassanai patted Keely's hand with his right. "Old Mr. Love will take care of you."

"Thank you," Keely said, then added, "Sir."

"No, you must call me Mr. Mitch. Yes?"

"Sure."

"You are beautiful," he said.

Despite everything that was happening, that was nice to hear.

They got to the back where a velvet rope hung between two stanchion posts. A man who could have been a Wall Street banker from the 1920s stood here. And smiled as they approached.

"Nice to see you again, sir," he said, extending his hand.

Al-Kassanai shook it. "Are the dice hot?"

"Like Krakatoa," the man said. And the two men laughed.

The banker unhooked the rope from one of the stanchions. As Al-Kassanai stepped through he said, "This is my lady."

"Welcome," the banker said with a nod and a knowing look.

"Thank you, I'm sure," Keely said.

The bodyguard followed. The banker replaced the velvet rope, then went to a door covered with fine leather and studs, and opened it.

"Good luck, sir," he said.

"She is my luck," Al-Kassanai, and led Keely through the door.

CHAPTER FORTY

TWO BIG CRAPS tables had action going on, along with three blackjack tables and a poker game. A couple of people greeted Al-Kassanai and he nodded to them with a big smile. There was a spot for him at the end of one of the craps tables. The table had blue felt and numbers and boxes all over it. Keely never really understood the game, except that it was good to roll a seven or eleven the first time out.

Al-Kassanai whispered something to his bodyguard. A cocktail waitress barely wearing a swimsuit style dress asked if she could bring them a drink. Al-Kassanai motioned for Keely to order. Keely said she'd like a Coke. Al-Kassanai ordered a Shirley Temple.

At this particular table stood three women, stunningly dressed, each beside one man. Keely figured the women as rentals. Just like her.

Mr. Bodyguard came back and placed some chips in the rail in front of Al-Kassanai. They were red and green and purple.

Kassanai handed Keely a purple chip. It had *50K* stamped on it. Al-Kassanai said that she should blow on the chip.

She did.

She handed the chip back to him and he tossed it on the table. "Any crap," he said.

The stickman slid the chip on to a letter C.

The man at the end of the table, gray-haired and wearing what he never should have—a black silk shirt with a gold chain around his neck—selected two dice off the table and rattled them in his hand. He tossed, and the dice padded across the table and hit the other side, right in front of Keely.

Snake eyes.

Al-Kassanai smiled as his dealer pushed a small stack of purple chips over to him.

"You are my lucky star," he said to Keely.

You better start losing, she thought.

Then she smiled and said, "Oh, Mr. Mitch."

She gave him a neck nuzzle.

He held his right fist up to her face. "Love is going to take care of you later."

THE ACTION WAS FAST. The voice of the stickman saying things like, "Eight the hard way" and "Ten easy" and "Aces" and "Center field."

The dice would go around and the people would get excited and say things to each other, and then there'd be a let down, "Craps, the loser."

When Al-Kassanai got the dice he would let Keely blow on them, and that was getting old fast, but she did it with a sultry pout. She'd clap her hands when Al-Kassanai won, and pretend to be sad when he lost.

Once he got angry with a dealer and they had some words, and then he lost about a hundred grand (if she was keeping track of the colors right) and threatened to leave the table. But she took his arm and said, "I like this. You can do it, Mr. Mitch." And she gave him a squeeze, licked her bottom lip and he smiled and motioned for his bodyguard to get more chips.

On and on it went with only a couple of short breaks to answer nature's call. Kassanai downed four espressos during their time at the table. Keely played the part of the dutiful eye-candy who everybody knew was eye-candy because that's what was sold in Las Vegas, Nevada.

And then came a bad run for Haji Zainul Al-Kassanai.

He told Keely she was getting cold, and he did not like it.

She told him to give her another chance.

She shifted from his left side to his right side.

It didn't help.

The chips on the rail disappeared.

Al-Kassanai said something in a language Keely did not recognize. He threw up his hands and turned away from the table.

Keely said, "No, please? Please, I like it."

He said, "You like to see me lose?"

"I like a comeback," she said. "You know, like in the movies." She wasn't thinking of any movie in particular. She just knew that Americans like a good comeback and Mr. Mitch liked American movies.

It worked.

He smiled and he nodded and he got more chips.

And the evening wore on.

It certainly seemed to Keely that he was losing more than he was winning. But she had done her job.

They had to take that into account. They had to get Ynez out of there. What more could Keely do?

Oh yeah, there was one more thing.

"Time for us to go get happy," Al-Kassanai said.

It was almost two a.m.

CHAPTER FORTY-ONE

THE VILLA WAS huge and plush. The floor was tiered so you had to walk down into the center of the room. A massive bar took up one whole side of the room.

And a water feature next to the windows that looked out at the sparkling Las Vegas night.

The bodyguard, whose name Keely still didn't know, made a quick turn around the place as Al-Kassanai stood smiling next her.

"Do you like?" he said.

"Couldn't you find anything bigger?" Keely said.

"That is what I like about you. You have a good American sense of humor. You are like one of those dolls from a Robert Mitchum movie."

Keely was starting to feel the drain. She had been on her feet for five hours watching this man roll "the bones," as he called the dice.

Yes, he'd lost a lot of money. But now his payoff was coming, and she was it.

The bodyguard approached and gave Al-Kassanai a nod. He reached into his pocket and pulled out a roll of currency. American. He peeled off what looked like two hundred-dollar bills and gave them to the bodyguard. The big man folded the money and placed it in his pocket, opened the door and left.

"It is time for love," Al-Kassanai said, once more holding up his stupid fist. And then he stood there as if he didn't know what to say or do. Like a schoolboy. As if he were waiting for her to make the first move.

Okay, Keely, you have done this hundreds of times. You know the deal, the role. And remember, this is for Ynez and Lucy.

"Where would you like it, Mr. Mitch," Keely asked in her sultry voice. She was a little out of practice, but thought she did all right.

"You will do anything I ask?" Al-Kassanai said.

"I'm all yours," she said.

"All?" he said.

Sheesh, what did he want? Twin bungee cords outside the hotel?

"It's your call," Keely said. "Only..."

"Yes?"

She put a hand on her throat. "I wish I was more dressed up for you, you know, diamonds and pearls."

Al-Kassanai nodded and wagged his finger at her. "If you please me, you will get rocks. That's what they call diamonds in the movies, isn't it?"

"I believe so. And if they are stolen, they are called hot rocks."

Al-Kassanai laughed and then placed his right hand fully on her throat.

And squeezed.

Keely batted his hand away. "I'm not into that."

"You said you would do anything," Al-Kassanai said.

"I draw the line right there."

"At pain?"

"That's right."

"Everything else?"

"What have you got lined up for me, baby?"

"You will see," he said.

She didn't like the sound of that. Her gymnastics days were over.

Al-Kassanai removed his coat and walked to the middle of the room where there was a large sofa. He tossed his coat onto a chair, sat on the sofa and motioned for her.

She walked toward him.

"Right there," he said.

She stopped.

"Now," he said, "you will take off your dress. Slowly, please."

Ah, the old striptease act. She'd done it many times with the sound of snare drums in her head.

And so she began.

Slowly.

He watched.

She made it slow.

He smiled.

She stepped out of her dress.

He put up his hand for her to stop.

He stood and removed his tie, then his vest.

Then unbuttoned his shirt halfway.

And started across the room.

Where was he going?

He turned and motioned for her to follow.

Ynez ... Lucy ...

She followed.

Into a massive bedroom. Low lighting. Sweet fragrance.

Too sweet.

Al-Kassanai was at the foot of the bed, beckoning her with his finger.

Geronimo. Bombs away. Here we go.

Keely took two steps and out of the corner of her eye saw something move.

She stopped.

There was a girl in the bed.

. . .

MAYBE TWELVE YEARS OLD.

Keely went cold all over.

She glared at Al-Kassanai. "No way."

"Eh?" he said.

"Uh-uh," Keely said.

"You have promised."

"Not this."

"There is no pain."

"She's not of age, man."

He came toward her then, his lips pursed in anger.

"You stupid," he said. "She is my wife."

The chill inside Keely went to absolute ice. Her mind whip-sawed ... *Ynez ... murder charge ... a girl in the bed ... she can't be his wife ... what if she is? ... it doesn't matter ... you can't do this ... you have to do this ... Lucy ... Lucy!*

The girl in the bed had wide, frightened eyes.

"You're lying," Keely said.

"No!" Al-Kassanai said. To the girl he said, "Tell her."

The little girl paused. Her eyes stayed the same. But she nodded.

"Count me out," Keely said. She walked out of the lavish bedroom, back into the stadium-like villa, and snatched her dress off the floor.

Al-Kassanai, moving faster than she'd anticipated, was suddenly there, and he grabbed the dress and pulled it from her hand.

"I own you tonight," he said.

"Give me my dress."

He held it up like a fish he's just caught. And smiled. "You are not going anywhere without this."

"Watch me," she said.

She started for the door. The odds were this wouldn't be the first time a woman in bra and panties was seen walking around a Las Vegas hotel.

She thought about finding a fire alarm to pull.

"Stop!" Al-Kassanai was at the door just as she got there.

Keely knew one jiu-jitsu move. A boy taught it to her when she was nine. He liked her and knew she was bullied, and he wanted to help. He showed her how to get up close and put her leg behind a person, then push hard in the chest.

Which is what she did to Al-Kassanai.

Who tumbled over her leg and hit the floor, his legs splayed.

She burst out into the corridor. The elevator was a million miles away. She ran for it.

And saw coming her way a security guy, dressed in black, shades and all.

Oh boy, what this must look like.

"Can you help me?" she said. "Please."

She looked behind her, expecting Al-Kassanai to come out.

"Easy," Security said. "Let's cover you up."

He took off his coat and put it around Keely's shoulders. She happily pulled it closed around her.

"Let's get out of here," Security said. With his arm around her he guided her to a hallway on the left, then through a door to a stairwell.

"It's all right now," he said.

Keely caught her breath.

"Thank you," she said to the security guy, who took off his shades.

"You're welcome, Keely," he said.

Then he put one hand over her mouth and the other on her throat.

CHAPTER FORTY-TWO

IT COULDN'T BE HIM.

But it was.

"I couldn't let you go," Rich said. "You mean too much to me."

He had her pinned against the wall. She could hardly breathe.

Next thing she knew they were out another door and onto a portion of the roof.

He let the door close, then pressed her against it.

"Take in the night air," he said. "We're going to enjoy it together."

She wanted to scream, to hit, to run, to lash out. But he had her under perfect control.

"I want you to know I've been living for this moment," he said. "You do something to me, Keely."

Did he want the phone? Was that what this was about? Was he going to thrash it out of her?

"I want you to know what you mean to me," he said. "I want you to see something."

Keeping his hand on her throat, he reached for something. Held it up to her.

The phone.

"I don't lose," he said. "And that's what makes you so worthy. But we don't have much time."

He put the phone in his pocket, then came back with something else.

Click.

A knife.

The point of it touching her left breast.

"This is a good place to die," he said. "What better place? You won't have to grow old. You shouldn't grow old."

She'd long thought she'd die young. But now she did want to live, to grow old.

There was nothing she could do.

She tried to move.

"You need to know something," he said. "As you slip away, know that I will be with you in the most intimate way. It's not an animal act, Keely. It's exaltation."

Forgive me, Ynez.

Forgive me, Lucy.

Forgive me, Noona.

I let you all down.

The knife pierced her skin.

Keely heard a thump.

And his head jerked to the side.

A warm spray hit Keely's face.

As his body crumpled at her feet.

What?

A scuffing sound.

In shock, Keely wanted to scream.

Brigita said, "Are you all right?"

SHE WAS HOLDING a pistol with a noise suppressor. In a stunning white evening dress.

"Do you know him?" Brigita said.

Keely couldn't speak. She touched herself above the breast. Felt a wetness.

"We need to take care of that," Brigita said.

"How ..."

Brigita bent over the body, quickly and efficiently going through pockets, removing items. She put them in the purse that had been around her shoulder.

What was going on? This woman was dressed like she was going to a movie premiere and she'd just blown a man's brains out.

"Can you walk?" she said.

"I think so," Keely said.

"Come."

Keely took a step then said, "Wait. Did you take his phone?"

"There are two of them."

"Good," Keely said.

THEY TOOK ANOTHER DOOR, for which Brigita had a mag key. Keely held her hand over her wound. Her hand was sticky with blood.

Brigita led her down a flight of stairs, through another door that required the card. The corridor was more like a hospital's, narrow.

Beauty with a handgun and silencer, Keely in scanties and bleeding. In a secluded section of a high-end hotel. And the body of her would-be killer on the roof.

Right.

What happens in Vegas is out-of-control weird in Vegas.

Another door. Inside a windowless room with cupboards, drawers, a sink.

And one of those doctor chairs with the paper on it.

"Sit," Brigita said.

Keely sat.

Her savior put her gun across the corner of the sink and opened a drawer.

And proceeded to clean and dress Keely's wound.

All while wearing a spotless white dress.

"Now can you tell me how you did that?" Keely said.

"Did what?"

"Showed up just in time to kill a guy who was going to kill me?"

"Ah," Brigita said. "Excuse me." She picked up a wall phone and punched in two numbers. A moment later she spoke. "We need Adam ... the roof, section seven ... yes ... thank you."

She came back to Keely and finished with the gauze and tape.

"So how did you do it?" Keely asked.

"I was watching you." Brigita said.

"Cameras?"

Brigita nodded.

"Not ... not even in that guy's room?"

"Even there."

"Creepy!" Keely said.

"Not at all," Brigita said. "Merely a precaution."

"Yeah, well, it's that Mitch guy who is the real creep."

"That is not for you to say." Brigita stepped back. "How does that feel?"

Keely touched her dressing. "Fine, I guess." She looked into Brigita's beautiful blue eyes. "You kill people?"

"I have," Brigita said.

"Why didn't you kill us both?"

"You? Why would I do that?"

"Because I blew it."

Brigita nodded. "That will be discussed later. Now let's see who this pro was."

"Pro?"

She held up a small black box about the size of a deck of cards. "He used this to disable the alarm on the roof-access door. He was planning to get you out there all the time."

"That little thing?" Keely said.

"This little thing is a very sophisticated jammer. It sends in radio noise to keep the signal from getting through from the sensors to the control panel. He had the equipment."

She took out items from her purse and placed them on the counter. A wallet, keys, and two phones.

"What do you know about him?" Brigita said.

"Just that he followed me from L.A. All to get his hands on this." She held up the phone.

"What is it?"

"It belonged to a trick who died on me. In a manner of speaking. Remember when I mentioned the name Pinky?"

"That was strange," Brigita said.

"That was the nickname he used with me. This is his phone. And it must have some killer stuff on it. But ... I left it with a computer guy, someone who works with my friend. You don't think ..."

Brigita thought a moment. "I suspect this computer person is dead."

Keely's heart dropped.

"I can't help anyone," she said.

"Perhaps you can," Brigita said.

Head reeling, Keely just looked at her.

"Let's have a look at that phone," Brigita said. "And get you something to wear."

CHAPTER FORTY-THREE

AN HOUR LATER, IN Brigita's formal office, Keely was wearing one of Brigita's "old things," a Versace midnight blue silk pantsuit. Brigita was at her desk, the most perfect desk Keely had ever seen. It sang feng shui. Every item on it, from the computer keyboard to the little Rock Juniper Bonsai tree, seemed to have been placed by the most efficient team of planners money could buy.

Which would not have surprised Keely. She was wearing perhaps two-thousand dollars of cast-off clothing.

Going through the wallet now, Brigita removed the driver's license. "Lawrence A. Whitney," she said. "Does that name mean anything to you?"

"Not a thing."

"Visa. American Express platinum card. LA Fitness member. That's it."

"Nothing else?"

"Cash. Let's see. Three hundred and ... twenty-seven dollars."

"He didn't have much."

"A pro never does. This license is probably fake."

"I want to know who hired him."

"Perhaps this will tell us." Brigita picked up Pinky's phone. She opened a side drawer and pulled out a couple of cables. She tried attaching one to the phone. It didn't work. She tried the other. It went in. She plugged the other end into a USB hub next to the computer.

Keely couldn't see the monitor, but she did see the screen color change as it reflected off the wall behind Brigita.

Brigita tapped the keyboard. Watched. Tapped again. Moved her mouse around. Tapped.

Waited.

Finally, Brigita, leaning close to the monitor, said, "Ah, it seems your computer fellow got through."

"He did?"

"It's unlocked. We can do a physical acquisition."

"What's that?"

"The physical store of the phone," Brigita said. "We can copy it, bit-for-bit, and see what's there. It's like little bits of DNA left at a crime scene."

Keely went to Brigita's side of the desk. The monitor showed a list of phone numbers surrounded by data marks like brackets and arrowheads.

Brigita pointed to the top of the list. "Look at that. He made and received lot of calls from this number," Brigita said. "That's where we should start."

"We?"

"I haven't got anything else to do at the moment," Brigita said. "And look here."

She pointed at some data set on the monitor. It looked like alphabet soup.

"These are deleted files," Brigita said.

"You can see them?"

"It's a beautiful thing, isn't it? They were not wiped from the memory."

Brigita clicked around with the cursor. "Ah, see?"

Within what looked like code were bits of readable text. But any coherent message was chopped up.

"Let me move some things around," Brigita said.

She went at it fast and sure, no hesitation. In addition to being the most beautiful woman in the world, she had technical precision and know-how. Keely wondered what she would look like in a Wonder Woman suit.

Then, without thinking about it, Keely put her hand on Brigita's shoulder. Brigita paused, looked back at Keely, and smiled. She patted Keely's hand in reassurance.

Five or ten minutes passed.

Keely had to sit back down. She was spent. All she wanted to do was sleep. And then wake up in her grandmother's house and be seven again.

"Now this is interesting," Brigita said. "Does the name Ali Botros mean anything to you?"

"No," Keely said.

"How about Tim McGinnis?"

"Uh-uh."

"Stuart Sunsten?"

"Not a clue."

"Well here's what I'm seeing," Brigita said. "Stuart Sunsten is the owner of this phone. He must be the one who called himself Pinky."

"He seemed fond of that name."

"To each his own," Brigita said. "Now ... most recently it seems he had some sort of deal going with this Ali Botros. An investment in a venture. Pinky looks like a major player."

"Something seems off to me," Keely said.

Brigita looked at her. "Tell me."

"I'm not sure."

"Think about it. You have a mind, put things together."

Keely said, "That's funny, the way you put it."

"What is?"

"Pieces together. Like a puzzle. I always liked puzzles."

"That's a good quality to have," Brigita said. "Life is pretty much all about figuring things out."

"Come to think of it," Keely said.

"So figure." Brigita sat back and folded her arms.

"Well, if this guy, this Botros, was doing business with Pinky, they'd probably have shared a lot of data."

"True."

"So it's not about discovering anything about Pinky himself."

"Keep going."

Keely paced in front of the desk. "Maybe there is some key information Pinky had that Botros needs. But ..."

"Yes?"

"It's unlikely Pinky kept something explosive on his phone. He wasn't one of those guys always looking at it. Just for basics."

Brigita nodded. She had a slight smile on her face, approving.

Keely said, "Maybe Botros thinks this phone could connect him to Pinky, and that's bad. Maybe that's why these messages were deleted."

"I'm sure of it. The phone had a secure passcode. That would have given Botros only slight comfort. He needs to be sure. He knows as well as you do now that nothing is impregnable."

Keely said, "Not even him."

"What's that?"

"He's not impregnated, either."

"I think you mean impregnable," Brigita said.

"Right. Tired."

"But finish the thought."

"If he wants this phone and this data to remain private, that puts me in the driver's seat."

"Brava," said Brigita.

"Maybe it's worth a lot of money to him."

Brigita smiled.

"Will you help me?" Keely said. "I mean, getting to this guy."

"This is as far as I can go," Brigita said.

Keely looked at the floor.

"Tell you what," Brigita said. "You need some sleep. There's a bed in the adjoining room. You go in there and I'll work up a few things here."

"Don't you need sleep?" Keely asked.

"No," Brigita said.

CHAPTER FORTY-FOUR

KEELY HAD ONE OF those dreams where she talked to herself in the dream, telling herself that it *was* a dream, but experiencing it as reality. How could she be back on the North Dakota playground as a little girl, her Noona watching and approving and smiling? And how could the black clouds gathering and the wind blowing not be making her run for cover? *Get out of there ... It's just a dream ... "Noona, watch me! I'm the queen monkey!"*

The jolt of wakefulness was like a slap.

"I'm sorry," a voice said.

Brigita.

Keely said, "What time is it?"

"A little after eight. Mr. Stoddard wants to see you."

"Stoddard?"

"He doesn't like to be kept waiting."

"YOU'VE CAUSED me a lot of trouble," Stoddard said. "I don't like trouble. I have to drink Pepto-Bismol when I have trouble."

"I'm not doing so good myself," Keely said. She was halfway presentable, but had a headache that would not quit.

Stoddard, seated at his desk, was clean and sharp. Like a knife.

"Can I remind you that you are not in any position to feel anything?" He said. "You made a deal to get me my money and you end up abusing a client?"

"Me? What about him? You approve of a three-way with a little girl?"

He slapped the desk. "At five grand an hour, you bet I approve. He can toss in a cage of squirrels if he wants to! And you don't get to say squat."

"Mr. Stoddard," Keely said, "I haven't said squat to many things in my life, but that has to be one of them."

"This is getting us nowhere," he said. "Your friend is going down, she's going away, her life is over. Her little girl isn't going to have a mommy. And you and your moral indignation can go on and be very happy together."

Keely said, "Please, wait."

"You had your chance. I don't give second chances."

"Please."

"You're through. And by the way, don't even think about trying to find a job here in Vegas. I will make sure no one hires you. The word will be out. So I suggest you leave town."

Keely felt herself getting sucked into darkness, into those black clouds she saw in the dream. She knew once inside she'd never get out. She had to grab on to something, or something had to grab on to her.

"If I may, Mr. Stoddard." It was Brigita. Keely had forgotten she was there.

"What is it?" he said.

"I'm wondering, there may be a way."

"No," he said. "No second chance."

"Ah," Brigita said, her voice cool and calm. "But what if we consider this part two of the first chance?"

Stoddard's right eyebrow arched.

"I've been looking at this phone data." Brigita held up her

tablet. "Whoever this man was, it is clear that he was quite wealthy. He has at least one offshore bank account. And he was a major investor in some sort of enterprise based in Los Angeles. There had to be a lot of money passing back and forth."

"And?" Stoddard said.

"It is big enough that this enterprise wants the data, and was going to kill Ms. Delmonico in order to get it. Which gives her a certain degree of leverage, if she knows how to use it."

Stoddard thought a moment, looked at Keely, back at Brigita. "You think she's up to it?"

"Up to what?" Keely said.

"The fine art of separating people from their money," Stoddard said. "I've been doing it all my life, in many different ways. You've only been doing it one way, the oldest way. But that's not going to be enough."

"Sir," Brigita said, "let me have some time with Ms. Delmonico. I can possibly suggest some things that might prove helpful."

Keely had no idea what that would be, but anything was better than the dismissal she'd just received, and the prospect of Ynez going to prison.

For a long moment Stoddard said nothing. He turned his chair around and looked out at the early morning darkness over Vegas. As if he himself could decide if the sun would come out again or not.

Finally he turned back and looked at Keely hard. "All right. Against my better judgment, I'm going to give you another shot."

"What about Ynez?" Keely said.

"What about her?" Stoddard said.

"She needs to be let go."

Stoddard shot to his feet. "She stays in jail until I get my money! And if I get tired of waiting, which will be in about five days, I write it all off as a loss. And watch your friend go down for spite. It'll be a great story for me to tell the next street trash that gets on my bad side."

Stoddard straightened his tie and sat back down. "I don't know what Brigita has in mind, but you can thank your lucky stars I trust her."

"I have lucky stars?" Keely said.

"Get her out of here," Stoddard said.

BRIGITA WALKED Keely back to her office. She took a moment to print out three pages from her computer. She handed them to Keely along with a flash drive that had the hotel logo printed on it.

"This is a summary of the important data," Brigita said. She pointed to a phone number at the top of the first page. "I suspect that this number will lead you to the man you need to talk to, a Timothy McGinnis, in order to get to the man who controls the money, Ali Botros. In other words, McGinnis is the man who is like I am to Mr. Stoddard. Use Pinky's phone to make the call. Make it from a random location. Then take the battery out of the phone."

"What should I say to this guy?"

"That's where you must use your insight into human behavior."

"I have insight into human behavior?"

Brigita smiled. "Your work experience guarantees it."

"Will you help me?" Keely said.

"I've done all I can."

"We could work together."

Brigita shook her head.

"But why?"

Into Brigita's eyes came a distant look. "Some things must be done alone, to get you where you must be."

She stayed in that far-off place for a moment, then came back to meet Keely's gaze.

"You can do this," Brigita said. "When the money is successfully transferred to our account, I will call you on your personal cell phone. And your friend will be released. Her alibi will be firmly established."

"Do you mind my asking," Keely said, "who is going to go down for the Buddy Ricks killing?"

Brigita said, "The answer is no one. It will be a cold case. Another tragedy in the City of Sin."

CHAPTER FORTY-FIVE

AT EXACTLY EIGHT A.M. Keely entered the North Las Vegas Detention Center. It took her twenty minutes to check in. She was told to wait until her name was called. It took ten years before someone finally called out *Kelly Delmico.*

Close enough.

She was buzzed into a room with cubicles. People were on phone handsets, looking at inmates on monitors.

How warm.

A scowling deputy nodded at Keely to take a seat at one of the cubicles.

Ynez was on the monitor, looking lost. Keely picked up her handset.

"I'm going to get you out," Keely said.

"How?"

"It may take a few days."

"My lawyer says they won't let me out on bail."

Your lawyer is a scum-sucking, lying lowlife, Keely thought, but said, "Let me try a few things."

"Like what?"

"Leave it to me."

"Don't do anything illegal," Ynez said.

"I said leave it to me," Keely said.

"I need to see Lucy."

"She's at Alma's."

"How much does she know?"

"Not all of it."

"Go ahead and tell her. Then bring her to see me."

AT ALMA'S, Keely took Lucy outside to talk.

"Honey, you know what jail is, right?"

Lucy nodded. "A place for bad people."

"That's right," Keely said. Time was moving faster than Keely ever thought possible. She needed to get to Los Angeles. She needed to do this thing before the fear caught up with her.

"But sometimes the police make a mistake," Keely said. "And they put a good person in jail. Then somebody has to fix something before the person can be let out."

"Is my mommy in jail?"

Sharp kid.

"Yes," Keely said. "And it's a great, big mistake."

Tears started to form in Lucy's eyes. Keely pulled Lucy to her.

"I'm going to try to fix the mistake," Keely said. "And get your mommy out."

"Is she scared?"

"A little. But you'll make her happy. Let's go see her."

"Yes!"

"VISITING HOURS ARE OVER."

The deputy sheriff who had taken over at the front desk was on the young side. But he'd already mastered the cold look of the immovable object. His nameplate said *Piese*.

Keely said, "This is her daughter. She hasn't seen—"

"I'm sorry, ma'am. Tomorrow you can bring her back."

"I want to see my mommy," Lucy said. If that pitiful voice couldn't crack this guy's heart, nothing could.

"Tomorrow," he said.

Okay, no crack in the heart.

"No," Keely said. "Now. I'm pretty sure that the local news would love to hear this story, and I'll be sure they get your name right, Officer ... is that pronounced peace or peez?"

He rolled his eyes. "You think you can threaten me?"

"No threat," Keely said. "It's an exercise of my first amendment right. The news is going to love a close-up of this little girl's face as she cries about Officer Peez who wouldn't let—"

"Peace," he said. "It's pronounced peace. And I'll give you five minutes."

DEPUTY PIESE shackled Ynez to the table, but allowed Lucy to put her arms around her mother's neck.

"I don't like it here," Lucy said.

"It will be all right," Ynez said.

"I want you to come home."

"I will."

"When?"

"Soon." Ynez looked at Keely with pleading eyes.

Deputy Piese looked at his nails.

ON THE DRIVE back to L.A. her body was tight, her head full of scenarios.

On the off chance there was a God and he was listening, maybe cutting her the break she didn't get as a kid, she told him she'd appreciate him making up for that oversight by making all this work, because Ynez needed to be out and Lucy needed Ynez. Come on, God, do me this solid and we'll call it even.

But the tightness stayed. The long stretch of desert highway went on and on.

CHAPTER FORTY-SIX

KEELY HIT THE 10 freeway a little before six.

The good news was it was Sunday, so there wasn't commuter traffic.

The bad news was that there was an accident that had things crawling through Upland, then another one in West Covina.

She didn't get to The Cognoscenti until seven-fifteen.

Amy saw her from behind the coffee bar. The look on Amy's face told Keely all she needed to know about what she must look like.

Keely dropped in a chair and tried to keep her head from spinning off its axis.

In ten seconds Amy was at her side.

"Where've you been?" Amy said.

"Give me a second."

"You look worried."

"Can you get me a coffee?"

"Sure, what'll you have?"

"Whatever's strongest."

"Be right back."

Keely took a deep breath and rubbed her eyes. When she

opened them again she met another set of eyes from across the shop.

It was that guy, Laptop Satan. What was his name again?

He smiled at her, nodded.

She felt like she owed him at least a nod. Wasn't he the one who told them that the cops had been there, asking to see her?

Traci. She made a mental note to call her.

Laptop Satan left his laptop.

Dang.

"Hey, where you been?" he said, pulling out a chair.

"Hi," she said.

He put on the charm, starting with a toothy smile. "I was hoping to see you again."

"Thanks," she said. "But I'm tired. Maybe another time."

"Sure, I'll call you."

"How about not?"

"Come on."

"I'm not interested," Keely said. "And I'm going to tell you the truth, okay? Really, this is it. It's not you, it's me."

"Oh, no."

"Yes, I'm giving you the *It's not you it's me* line. But you know why it's a line? Because sometimes it's true."

"I'm not giving up," he said.

"Look, you're moving from talking to stalking."

"That's not very nice."

"*I'm* not very nice, okay? Now please leave."

He stood, and kept smiling. "This isn't over."

"Yes, it is."

He shook his head as he went back to his laptop, which was one relationship he could control.

Amy came back with the coffee.

"Just in time," Keely said.

"What happened?"

"My fan." Keely nodded across the room.

After a glance at him, Amy said, "He's harmless. Annoying, but harmless."

"I'm ready for invisible," Keely said. She took a sip of coffee. It was hot and dark. "Can I sleep on your sofa tonight?"

"Yeah, sure. But what is going on?"

"I can't give it all to you," Keely said.

"Now you're making me want to know everything," Amy said.

"Can you trust me for a little while?"

"You know I will. As long as you tell me the whole thing someday."

"Yes."

"Soon!"

"I promise."

Keely took another sip of coffee. She saw Laptop Satan stealing a glance at her.

"I need to go outside," Keely said.

"Let's go," Amy said.

"Give me a few minutes," Keely said. "I have to make a call."

CHAPTER FORTY-SEVEN

SHE TOOK OUT PINKY'S phone and dialed the number of the guy named McGinnis.

Someone answered, but did not say anything.

"Your guy is dead," Keely said.

Silence.

"Whitney, that was his name, right?" Keely said.

"Who is this?"

"Shut up and listen. I've got Sunsten's phone. You know that. And all the data. It's really interesting reading. You want to listen now?"

No answer.

"Good," Keely said. "Because it's going to cost you. It's going to cost you a mil. Is there any part of a mil you don't understand?"

No answer.

Keely said, "When I ask you a question, you answer. Do you understand? Or shall I tell Ali Botros you're blowing it?"

After a long pause, the voice said, "Go on."

"One million dollars. I'll tell you where to transfer it. When the transfer is complete, the phone goes in a safe deposit box with all the transcribed data. If something should happen to me, even a bad cold that leads to my death, I have arranged for the information to be released to the FBI. That stands for Federal Bureau of Investigation. Also, the–"

"If I may?"

"Go for it, Tim."

"You don't have any idea what you're doing."

"I think I do, Tim. I can almost hear the sweat dripping under your arms."

She tried to ignore the rivulets streaking down both her sides.

He said, "I tell you, don't do this."

"You're not giving the advice here, Tim. I don't think Botros would approve."

Nothing.

"You there, Tim?"

"Go on."

Keely looked at one of the pages Brigita had printed for her.

"Let's see," she said. "I have some other names here. Do you know a Mr. Burton Horn?"

To Keely, the quiet on the other end seemed charged with explosives.

"Or Mr. Seth Lakey? He's a Los Angeles County Supervisor, isn't he?"

"How did you ... where did you–"

"Gene Montoya, Garry Arnold."

"Stop! You don't realize!"

"Realize what?"

"That you're dead."

She took a deep breath, and kept hold of her inner ninja. "The walking, talking dead who can eat your brain, friend."

Silence.

"Tim, I'm getting tired of kicking your butt, so I'll make it plain. You will do exactly what I tell you, and if you do, the information I have will remain a private little conversation between you and me."

Nothing.

"Help me out by breathing, Tim."

"What do you want?"

"I am going to give you the number of an offshore bank account. You will transfer one million dollars and five cents into that account."

"Five cents?"

"That's my carrying charge."

"What?"

"I'm messing with you, Tim, because I like it. Because you sent a guy to kill me and I don't like you for that."

"What you're asking is impossible."

"So be it, Tim. I don't mind dying. In fact, it will prove to be very restful. But before I do I'll take you and Botros and seventeen other names down with me. I have a feeling, too, that there will be other people who die, including you, Tim. So call it."

Silence.

"I'll start humming the *Jeopardy* theme now," Keely said "Dum duh dee dum—"

"Enough!"

"Let's wrap this up."

"What you're asking can't be done."

"Yes it can, Tim. And it will be done. By close of business tomorrow. I'll be monitoring the account. Write this information down."

When he said nothing, Keely gave him the bank transfer information. Not once did he speak. Until she was finished.

"I'll see what I can do," McGinnis said. "And call you."

"You won't be able to, Tim. I'm shutting down this phone. I will only be checking for the bank transfer."

"You're not being reasonable," McGinnis said.

"I know," Keely said. "You threw reason out the window when you tried to kill me."

"Maybe we can work something out," McGinnis said. "Between us."

"Sure, Tim. Maybe we could get married, too."

"I mean it. There's lots of room here. We should meet."

"Right."

"In a public place."

"Sure. I'll walk right in wearing bright colors. I wouldn't want your sniper to miss."

"You don't understand. We can both get what we want out of this."

"Not interested. I know what I want, and so do you. By close of business."

"Don't hang—"

Keely hung up.

She shut off the phone and took out the battery and threw the parts in her purse.

She looked out the window at the skies above Los Angeles. They were hazy but full of a glowing backlight. The sun was trying to break through.

CHAPTER FORTY-EIGHT

TIME TO KILL IN L.A.

Keely was at once happy and blue about it. Happy because this was like being back home. Even with all she'd been through and done here, she loved Los Angeles. There was something about it that embraced you, told you whatever happened you could get through it. All you had to do was drive and you'd end up somewhere healing.

At the beach at sunset.

In the Hollywood Hills when the view was clean.

Eating at a new restaurant where the conversation flowed.

A concert at the Bowl. A walk in Griffith Park.

But it was a blue city, too, where dreams died hard and people often wandered, lost, over sidewalks with stars on them.

And when there's unfinished business of the sort Keely had, the place could feel like it was closing in on you with its faux-friendly face.

Keely decided to take Mulholland Drive over to the Valley. There were some nice turnouts there where you could see the biggest suburban bowl in the world and think about nothing. Just look. And feel, for a few minutes at least, like you were high enough that nothing could touch you.

It was in just such a turnout that Keely stopped and thought about Traci Fears and her battering boyfriend Jimmy Hansen. Had Traci been able to do anything about it? Keely used her own phone to call her.

It went to voicemail.

"Hey, just checking on you, kid," Keely said. "Call me when you get the chance."

But as soon as she hung up she wondered if that chance would come.

What condition might she be in?

Keely's mind was going to all the wrong places. She tried to reason that this was because of her own condition, not Traci's, which she didn't know.

But dread was in the passenger seat next to her.

And it wouldn't get out.

Her phone bleeped. It was a text from Traci.

WHERE ARE YOU?

KEELY TEXTED BACK: *Back in LA. How are you?*

TRACI: *Not so good. But, y'know...*

KEELY: *No! Can I come over?*

TRACI: *Sure.*

KEELY STARTED THE CAR. From one crisis to the next, huh? That was the way it was going to be back in the blue city.

CHAPTER FORTY-NINE

TRACI FEARS LIVED IN an apartment building on Yucca. It was just about on the border between what the city fathers hoped would be the "new Hollywood" and the old. The old was decrepit and in various states of decline. The new was represented by the Highland center from which all things grand were supposed to emanate.

The problem was the emanations went only a couple of blocks each way.

From the street in front of Traci's building, you could smell both renewal and despair. You could see a neighborhood hipster walk by a neighborhood homeless man. Or a couple pushing a baby carriage passing a juice-head pushing drugs.

This time Keely didn't care who she saw. She just wanted to get up to see Traci.

The apartment door was being held open by a black woman talking to someone inside.

Keely said, "Excuse me," and stepped past the woman, who paid her no mind.

Welcome back to L.A.

Traci's apartment was on the first floor, at the end of the corridor.

The door was open a crack.

"Traci?"

Keely pushed the door, stepped inside.

"Hey, I'm here."

She walked into the small living room, saw nothing.

"Yo! Traci!"

Heavy steps from the kitchen. Keely turned.

And saw a uniformed police officer.

"What is your name, please?" the officer said. He was about forty, tall and trim.

"What is this?" Keely said.

"Do you know the party who lives here?"

"Where is she?"

"Your name and your relationship," he said.

"Keely Delmonico. I'm a close friend. She texted me to come over. What's wrong?"

"Come with me, and don't touch anything," the officer said.

He turned and started for Traci's bedroom.

Keely felt dread creeping up.

Please don't let her be dead.

The bedroom door was open. The cop went in.

Keely followed.

Traci was on the bed. Fully clothed. Not moving.

No, please ...

She tried to see if Traci was breathing.

Then Keely's own breathing stopped as something big and wet covered her nose and mouth.

CHAPTER FIFTY

SHE WAS HAVING TROUBLE coming out of the darkness.

A medicine smell lingered in her nose.

She didn't notice any pain. Just a heaviness of head and thought.

Her face rubbed against something soft.

Carpet?

She was on the floor?

Yes, a floor.

Light, there was light.

Then a voice.

"You have made me a lot of trouble."

A man's voice.

"You must be smart."

Keely turned her head – it was like pushing a small boulder in mud – and saw shoes. Black and shiny.

Ankles. No socks.

Slacks.

A red shirt, tight on a body.

A dark face, dark eyes, black hair.

"I don't like smart women. Always trouble. When I take a woman I want to know she won't be trouble after."

Take?

She was on the floor. Fighting for breath, she pushed herself to a sitting position. She looked around.

This was not Traci's apartment.

"Where ... is this?" she said.

"Your new home," the man said.

She looked into his mocking eyes.

"Botros," she said.

He smiled.

He was sitting in a soft-leather chair. The walls were painted a pastel shade of pink, like cotton candy. A framed poster of the Chrysler Building hung on the wall directly behind Botros. It looked like the Art Deco cap and spire were growing up out of Botros's head.

"There was a king of Persia," he said, "who kept one of his women on a leash. She was his tiger. You're going to be my tiger."

Blood rushing to her head, and the pumping of fear and help-lessness, cleared her mind. Her body was another matter. It was hard to move. She wanted to stand, couldn't.

"You'll like it here," he said. "I'll feed you and see that you get plenty of play time. Do you like to play, Keely?"

"Just shut up," she said. It was a feeble, powerless thing to say. It made her feel like when she was in elementary school, saying those very words to the girl bullying her. How the girl laughed.

As Botros did now.

"The tiger meows," he said. "There are a few things you need to know before we begin."

Begin?

Botros stood. "First of all, no money has been transferred, and never will be. Second, I have the phone and all the information, and I don't believe you're able to release that information. I believe you are all bluff. It was a good bluff, which is why I've kept you alive until now."

Survival instinct kicked in and she struggled to her feet. But there was no way out. He was physically stronger than she was. He would be able to counter her every move. Behind him and to the right was the start of a hallway. It undoubtedly led to the front door, because behind and to the left was a sliding glass door. Outside that door was a balcony.

And the lights of the city beyond.

Killer view.

"So we will get to know each other for a few hours," Botros said. "And then we can have a little meeting to decide what to do next."

Then he pulled off his shirt.

He had dark skin and eight-pack abs. The finest body money-for-a-trainer could buy.

Of course.

He was showing her there was nothing she could do, nowhere she could go. He would do to her whatever he wanted.

She thought about screaming. But she knew he'd be on her immediately, violently. Her only hope was to keep things slow and hope some way out would present itself.

A hope without any basis in reality.

"You'll like it if you relax a little," Botros said.

He took a step toward her. There was a glass coffee table between them, a sofa on her left. She moved a step toward it.

"Go ahead, fight it," he said. "I like it that way."

He made a sudden move. Like he was going to pounce.

Keely jumped back.

But it was only a fake.

Which made him smile.

He moved now around the coffee table.

Keely matched him step for step, to the back of the sofa.

There was nothing to grab, nothing to hit with.

The kitchen was across the room but there was too much space to cover. He'd be all over her before she could find a knife or glass or anything.

"Let me hear you snarl," Botros said.

He would be around the sofa with his next step.

With a lunge, Keely tried to open the sliding glass door.
Locked.

Botros laughed. "Go ahead," he said.

She flipped the lock. Slid the door open.

What was she thinking? Jump?

Maybe that would be better than what he had in store.

No.

Grab a chair.

There were two of them out there, with a table. A bistro set.
Probably some sort of aluminum. She grabbed one of the chairs
and held it up like a lion tamer.

Botros was in the door now, leaning, his right arm extended
upward against the inset.

"Watch it," he said. "That might hurt."

Keely backed up a few steps until she felt the balcony edge on
her butt. She gave a quick glance down. Car miniatures with toy
lights pulled up to a red stoplight.

"Twenty-two floors," Botros said.

Her hands began to tremble, her grip on the chair loosening.
Her body betraying her.

When he was within striking distance she put everything she
had into a thrust. It had the force of a butterfly. Botros snatched
the chair from her and threw it aside.

Then he was at her, chest to breast, his face an inch from hers.

His breath stank of garlic and chili peppers.

Putting one hand on her throat, he said, "I own you."

Keely looked at his eyebrows to avoid his eyes.

"You are mine," he said.

She closed her eyes.

Botros squeezed her throat. "Tell me you are my mine."

Keely tried to move her head.

Botros held it fast.

"Tell me," he said.

"No," Keely said, though her voice was constricted by his hand.

"No?" he said. "Just who do you think you are?"

And that's when she knew who she was. She felt herself smile, felt sunlight fill her with heat and energy ... she wrapped her arms around his waist, dug her fingers under his belt, gripped them like the reigns of a horse. Gripped them and pulled with all her might, her body behind the pulling as she thrust her legs upward and leaned her body backward, pulling, and his body thumped against her as they were, for a moment, face to face. Then gravity took over and she was falling downward as his body, unable to resist the physics of it, slid over her face, his belt buckle catching her nose, scraping it. And then he was gone, screaming in shock and outrage, and Keely heard it all, her legs hooked on the railing of the balcony, hanging there upside down, hearing a distant crunch.

Her body strong and exhilarated, Keely reached up to the ledge with her right hand, twisted, pulled herself up and over to safety. Like a lioness after a fresh kill, she wanted to roar, and looked down and said, "I am the Queen Monkey, that's who I am!"

A voice behind her said, "Shut up."

CHAPTER FIFTY-ONE

KEELY SPUN AROUND.

It was the cop from Traci's. Only he wasn't in uniform. He wore business casual. And had a gun.

"If you want to get out of this alive," he said, "do exactly what I say."

Keely's internals crashed then, her nerves and her blood. From survival to this.

"No way," she said.

"You've got to come with me now," the fake cop said, with evident surprise at her reluctance.

"You're going to have to shoot me."

"You want your money, don't you?"

She cocked her head.

"You'll get your money," he said. "But we've got to get out of here. This place is going to be crawling with cops."

"Who are you?"

"McGinnis. You can call me Tim. And you can trust me."

"You're kidding, right?"

"Does it look like I'm kidding?" he said. "Let's go."

Whatever! He took her to the elevator and down to the parking garage. His car was a red Corvette. He tore out of the garage and aimed for the freeway.

"Do you believe in Karma?" McGinnis said.

"No," Keely said.

"Neither do I. But sometimes things work out the way they should. The guy I worked for, the guy you just killed, is—was—Ali Botros. Comes from a family with big Saudi money. I know where the money is. We've got to move fast to get it."

"We?"

"You want that transfer, right?"

"Why would you do that now?"

"I know who I'm dealing with," McGinnis said. "Let's just say it's better to pay him off. I'm satisfied with what I'm getting."

"Who are you? Who was Botros?"

"I can tell you. We were going to be the Uber of prostitution."

"That's what all this was about? Prostitution?"

"It's a growth business," McGinnis said.

"But the killings?"

"You have to break some eggs to make an omelet."

"You killed people I was close to."

"I didn't," McGinnis said.

"You hired a hit man."

"He was only supposed to get the phone. You made it more complicated."

"You're blaming me?"

McGinnis shrugged.

Keely said, "Somebody's got to pay for all this."

"Already paid, right? Botros and Whitney are dead."

"You're not."

"You can be glad about that. This makes us even."

"How do you figure?"

"Because, like everything else in life, it comes down to who controls the money. I do, and I say we're even."

"What are you going to do next?"

"Probably spend some time on the beach in Cabo. They could

use my services down there. What about you? You going to continue in your chosen profession?"

And then Keely knew.

"I'm going to get into real estate," she said.

"Good choice," McGinnis said. "Sell houses instead of your body. Better future. Where can I drop you?"

"Just like that?"

"Just like that. Life is funny that way."

"I just decided I do believe in Karma," Keely said. "Because justice has to bite you in the butt someday."

"I'll keep an eye on where I sit," McGinnis said.

"How can I trust you about the money?" Keely said.

"You don't really have a choice, do you? But if you'll give me a couple of hours, you'll know."

SHE ASKED him to drop her at Farmer's Market on Fairfax. She went to DuPar's. It was a place she often went in her—now—other life. Late night pancakes, soaked in butter. Nothing better for the empty stomach and even the empty soul.

She ordered a short stack and coffee and sat at the counter watching the people.

Normalcy again.

And once again, she wondered if she could fit it.

She had two refills of coffee after finishing the pancakes. Then she strolled around the market, occasionally looking at the time.

At 3:35 her phone buzzed.

"Hello, Keely."

Brigita.

"What's going on?" Keely said.

"It is done. Your friend is being released even as we speak."

Keely's sigh startled a little girl standing at a candy counter.

"Is that it, then?" Keely said.

"It is," Brigita said. "Mr. Stoddard is satisfied. No debt remains."

"Unbelievable," Keely said. She had to fight back the emotion trying to break through her chest and onto her face.

"Good luck in your life," Brigita said.

"Will I ever see you again?" Keely said.

"You never know."

CHAPTER FIFTY-TWO

TWO WEEKS LATER Keely was in the front row of the courtroom of Judge Melinda Marvin of the Los Angeles County Superior Court. Traci Fears was seated next to her. Keely held Traci's trembling hand as the judge—an African American woman in her fifties—called to order Traci's hearing for a restraining order against Jimmy Hansen.

On the other side of the courtroom sat Hansen himself, dressed like a choir boy. No doubt at the urging of his lawyer, a big timer named Bruce Spangler. Next to Jimmy was his agent, Tad Bullock, whose expression was as sour as an unripe grapefruit. But his eyes were flamethrowers when he looked at Keely.

She smiled at him.

The rest of the courtroom was filled almost to capacity. There were at least two reporters present. A woman in a coat with an ESPN logo, and a guy with a pad and pen wearing a TMZ T-shirt.

"In the matter of Traci Fears," the judge said. "Ms. Fears, are you ready to proceed?"

Traci and Keely stood.

"Yes, Your Honor," Traci said.

"I understand you wish to represent yourself?"

"Yes, ma'am. I mean, Your Honor."

"I strongly advise against it," Judge Marvin said. "The other party is well represented. If you would like some more time to consult with an attorney, the court will grant it."

Keely heard herself say, "She's ready now, Your Honor."

"Excuse me," said the judge. "You have not been recognized by the court. Ms. Fears, who is this?"

"My friend, Keely Delmonico. I've asked her to assist me."

The silver-haired lawyer Bruce Spangler stood and said, "We object, Your Honor. Ms. Delmonico is not an attorney, and cannot speak for anyone in a court of law."

"But I'm not—" Keely started to say.

"Ms. Delmonico," said Judge Marvin, "you will not speak unless called on by me, understood?"

"Yes," Keely said. "I mean ..." and she nodded.

"All right," Judge Marvin said. "You understand you are not representing Ms. Fears, correct?"

Keely nodded.

"You can answer out loud now," said the judge with a slight smile.

"Oh. Yes."

"In what way are you assisting Ms. Fears?"

"Mostly just being here for her."

"More like a support?"

"Well, yes, I suppose."

"You keep supposing that," Judge Marvin said. "Nothing wrong with a supporter, is there Mr. Spangler?"

"But she is also being called as a witness," Spangler said. "Which makes her presence a conflict of interest."

Judge Marvin looked at Keely. "I don't suppose you've got an answer for this, do you, Ms. Delmonico?"

"If I may, Your Honor," Keely said. "It's true I'm not an attorney, but I've seen a ton of episodes of *Law & Order*."

The people in the gallery laughed.

"What I mean," said Keely, "is that when a lawyer makes an

objection, he should be able to give you a ... what's it called ... a sedation?"

"You mean citation?" said the judge.

"That's it!" Keely said.

The courtroom laughed again.

"Quite right," Judge Marvin said. "Mr. Spangler, do you have a citation for me?"

Spangler cleared his throat. "Well, if Your Honor needs one, I can certainly look for one."

"Objection overruled," Judge Marvin said. "Let's move this thing along. Ms. Fears, if you'll come forward and take the stand."

Traci gave her testimony. She held up well under Bruce Spangler's questioning, with help from Judge Marvin, who kept the lawyer's histrionics in check.

Then it was Keely's turn. The judge questioned her and Keely told about her encounter with Tad Bullock, and then Jimmy Hansen's stalking her in the parking garage, and tweaking her cheek. Spangler moved to have the testimony stricken. Judge Marvin denied the motion.

After Keely stepped down, the judge asked Spangler if he had anything to offer. Spangler, Jimmy Hansen, and agent Tad Bullock huddled. Then Spangler said, "We're ready to submit this, Your Honor." He then spent fifteen minutes giving his argument why the restraining order should be denied.

The judge granted it.

That evening several news outlets reported that both UCLA and the NFL were looking at the Hansen matter. TMZ reported that if Hansen dropped in the draft because of this, it could cost him at least twenty million dollars.

Keely experienced the best sleep she'd had in months.

THREE WEEKS AFTER THAT, Keely Delmonico sat at her favorite table at Cognoscenti, sipping coffee and using a yellow highlighter on a book called *How to Get Started in Real Estate*.

Normalcy. And a goal. A new life. It all felt so good.

Even with Laptop Satan at an adjoining table, tossing looks her way as she spoke to Ynez on the phone.

"Yes, I'm serious," Keely said. "And when I get my license, it sure would be nice to have a partner."

"Have anybody in mind?" Ynez said.

"Ha ha."

"You ready to move to Las Vegas?"

"How about you and Lucy to L.A.?"

"Ack!"

"Let's sell some houses."

"One step at a time, girl. I just came out of a meeting at my office. The higher ups think this virus thing is going to hit the housing market it a big way."

"You mean that virus from China?"

"Yep."

"But it's just like the flu, right?"

"They say it's worse."

"Come on now," Keely said. "Are we going to let a little thing like that stop us?"

Ynez laughed. "I don't think anything's going to stop you from now on."

"You got that right," Keely said.

WHEN SHE PUT the phone down, Keely saw Laptop Satan staring at her. He started to get up.

She narrowed her eyes and wagged her finger at him.

He sat back down.

The Queen Monkey did not wish to be disturbed.

AUTHOR'S NOTE

Many thanks for reading *Last Call*. I greatly appreciate it. Added appreciation would come if you would kindly leave a review on the Amazon site. For ebook readers, the link to do so is below (you may be asked to sign in to your Amazon account).

Leave a review for Last Call

Again, thank you! And please read on to see more of my thrillers.

If you are a writer, I've written a lot on the craft of popular fiction. You'll see links for my books on writing, and my online teaching, at my website:

JamesScottBell.com

MORE THRILLERS FROM JAMES SCOTT BELL

The Mike Romeo Thriller Series

Romeo's Rules
Romeo's Way
Romeo's Hammer
Romeo's Fight
Romeo's Stand

"Mike Romeo is a terrific hero. He's smart, tough as nails, and fun to hang out with. James Scott Bell is at the top of his game here. There'll be no sleeping till after the story is over." - **John Gilstrap**, New York Times bestselling author of the Jonathan Grave thriller series

The Ty Buchanan Legal Thriller Series

#1 Try Dying
#2 Try Darkness
#3 Try Fear

"Part Michael Connelly and part Raymond Chandler, Bell has an excellent ear for dialogue and makes contemporary L.A. come alive. Deftly plotted, flawlessly executed, and compulsively readable. Bell takes his place as one of the top authors in the crowded suspense genre." - **Sheldon Siegel**, *New York Times* bestselling author

The Trials of Kit Shannon Historical Legal Thrillers

Book 1 - City of Angels
Book 2 - Angels Flight
Book 3 - Angel of Mercy
Book 4 - A Greater Glory
Book 5 - A Higher Justice
Book 6 - A Certain Truth

"With her shoulders squared and faith set high, Kit Shannon arrives in 1903 Los Angeles feeling a special calling to practice law ... Packed full of genuine, deep and real characters ... The tension and suspense are in overdrive ... A series that is timeless!" — **In the Library Review**

Stand Alone Thrillers

Your Son Is Alive
Blind Justice
Don't Leave Me
Final Witness
Framed

Mallory Caine, Zombie-At-Law Series

You read that right. A new genre. Part John Grisham, part Raymond Chandler—it's just that the lawyer is dead. Mallory

Caine, Zombie at Law, defends the creatures no other lawyer will touch...and longs to reclaim her real life.

Pay Me In Flesh
The Year of Eating Dangerously
I Ate The Sheriff

ABOUT THE AUTHOR

 **James Scott Bell** is a bestselling author of thrillers and books on the writing craft. He is a winner of the International Thriller Writers Award and the Christy Award (Suspense). He studied writing with Raymond Carver, graduated with honors from USC Law School, and practiced law with a large litigation firm before beginning his writing career. He lives and writes in Los Angeles.

JamesScottBell.com

Follow JSB on BookBub

Made in the USA
Monee, IL
23 October 2020